WEST PAC

WEST PAC

"Enlisted men are stupid, but they are sly and cunning and bear considerable watching."

-Navy Officer's Guide, 1894

GEORGE YENNEY

EDITED BY: ALEX YENNEY

WEST PAC

This is a work of fiction. All of the characters, names, incidents, organizations, and dialogue in this novel are either the products of the author's imagination or are used fictitiously.

iUniverse books may be ordered through booksellers or by contacting:

iUniverse LLC
1663 Liberty Drive
Bloomington, IN 47403
www.iuniverse.com
1-800-Authors (1-800-288-4677)

ISBN: 978-1-4917-4498-7 (sc)
ISBN: 978-1-4917-4499-4 (e)

Library of Congress Control Number: 2014915161

Printed in the United States of America.

iUniverse rev. date: 09/03/2014

CONTENTS

For my daughter and son.

"Don't talk to me about naval tradition,
it's all rum, sodomy and the lash"
-Winston Churchill

PROLOGUE

Topa, the old stores ship, cut through the bright blue swells of the Tonkin Gulf at fourteen knots. She vibrated violently, the ocean's whiteness exploding at her bow, gray smoke billowing from her gray stack. Two ships had just broken away from her, left like sailors on liberty would leave a prostitute and returned to the line to shell Viet Cong position on the coast in support of ground operations. Topa was like an old sea going whore that served the fleet, and she was about to accept two more lovers. The foreplay had begun. This time they were destroyers, "tin cans" in Navy parlance, and made their approaches like dogs to a bitch in heat, carefully from the rear. The tin cans pitched and rolled wildly as they came within range, close enough to receive shot lines from the old girl. The Topa's P.A. system blared.

"NOW STANDBY TO RECEIVE SHOT LINES FORE AND AFT. ON DECK TAKE COVER!" The tin can's deck apes scurried for cover on the lee side of her guns and superstructure as the line guns boomed and carried the monkey fists whirling toward them. As the monkey fists bounced on the deck, the apes scampered to recover the lines before they were pulled back over the side. The underway replenishment had begun.

High on the side of the superstructure of the ship, in forbidden Officer's Country, skivvy wavers attempted, by unauthorized hand and arm semaphore, to contact someone from their hometowns on the closing ships. Is there anybody on you from Des Moines, Mobile, or Cheektowaga? The answers came back. What school did you go to, Central or North? Do you know this girl or that? Yes, she married my best friend home on leave.

Down in the engine room the black gang watch standers, in old dirty grimy dungarees peered through the polluted 130-degree heat waves to monitor ancient gauges as the old lady trembled along.

On the bridge, the Captain stared down on his command, and his underway watch steadied the ship, striving to maintain course and speed and the scant distance between the three ships, willing nobody would lose steering and cause a collision. A collision, no matter whose fault, would be career ending.

On the main deck, Topa's deck apes worked frantically to get the ships hooked together. Lines and cargo booms were readied. The men stood by to take the cargo, some already in netted pallets on the deck, some being made up deep in the holds, and transfer the loads to the other ships.

Down below the main deck, below the water line, in the depths of the cargo hold, men worked. They were stripped naked to the waist. In dungarees and hard hats they sweated profusely in the tropic South East Asian heat. These apparitions were caked with the white wheat flour, making race or creed indeterminable. They humped cargo as fast as they could, grunting and swearing. From the dark humid stifling depths of the hold to the swaying light of the hatch square, the goods flowed. The boxes and bags were loaded onto pallets that had been set on cargo nets. New item names and quantities were called out and the frantic search for their location began. During this reprieve in the work the men paused, sucking big gulps of polluted air, their chests heaving deeply, sweat poured down their flour caked bodies. They'd been at it since pre reveille darkness. Once the new item was found the screaming and grunting started again as the cargo was passed from man to man from the depth of the hidden dark recesses of the hold to the light of the hatch square. When the pallet was full, the corners of the cargo net were slung on the cargo hook and the signal was given for the net to be hoisted away. Grinding winches pulled it up. Men cleared the hatch area, scurrying for cover under the holds eves as the cargo net swung to the top of the hold's mouth and blotted out the sun.

One man stayed looking up toward the eclipsed light at the top of the hold. Then the sirens of emergency break away sounded. Loud, short, ugly blaring screams from the ship's horn. One of three ships had lost her steering. Tons moving at 14 knots had swung out of control.

The men deep in the hold, below the main decks and the water line, stopped and listened to the slosh of the sea running along their ship and eyed the long narrow rung of steel ladders that ran to the main deck. They knew there was danger. They knew they could be trapped.

The sailor was knocked to the deck by the impact of the two vessels. He saw from the depths the pallet collide with the side of the hold. The net broke open. In slow motion the cargo poured out of the net and pelted him to the deck. He tried to move but couldn't. The ship heeled over. Emergency break away echoed again.

CHAPTER 1

Reporting Aboard, Alameda 1969

I saw her along the pier, among the other gray vessels, an old five hold auxiliary cargo ship of WWII vintage, humming and buzzing softly in the swirling thick fog of the east San Francisco Bay. She both beckoned and warned me in the yellow pier lights. Her bow, now and then obscured by the cold wind driven silver gray fog faced Asia. I flipped the dark green sea bag off my right shoulder single handedly and landed it upright on the cement with a thud. I adjusted my white hat the regulation two fingers width above my eyebrows and fastened the top button of my dark navy blue pea coat against the moist chill. My left hand remained motionless at my side clutching the sealed manila envelope that contained my records and orders. I looked at my new ship.

The TOPA was a gray U.S. Navy vessel with her superstructure amid ship and a raised forecastle. There was a big empty gun tub aft. She was tied to the pier with standard crisscross lines that were protected by aluminum rat guards. A tangle of booms, spread over the pier like a spider's web, had been taking on cargo. She lay low in the water, almost fully loaded, ready for another deployment to the far Pacific, to the coast of Vietnam, a West Pac Cruise. I would be riding her back to Asia soon.

The only thing I'd been able to find out about her was from a casual conversation with a retired sailor who had seen her. A dirty ship, he'd said, and a hard working one. I closed my eyes and tried to separate her buzz from the other ships along the pier. I was like a baby bird trying to imprint on my new mother or a baby listening to the hum of mother's breathing, the thump of her heart. Tonight I would fall asleep to her lullaby. I would be inside her.

I had been to Vietnam before: a one year long plus tour on the beach humping ammo. Da Nang, and Hue. From May to November 68' I served on a San Diego home ported tender, making my crow, becoming a petty officer third class. Almost as soon as I had made it, I'd been transferred north. My time was short in the Navy. This would be my last deployment, unless I shipped over.

I'd spent the last ten days on transit leave, mostly riding the lonely waves of Ventura County. I looked for old friends at home but more than three years away had changed a lot of things. Most of the guys I had surfed with had disappeared. I had no idea where most had gone. I had seen Darrel, a chance meeting as I loaded him, badly wounded, into a medevac helicopter at the imperial Capitol of Hue. Gene was in college at Washington State. Pete had gone to Canada and his brother to Vietnam. The casual friends I had known from surfing, those who remembered me, I simply lied to, telling them I had been working in San Diego for the past three years. It was easier than answering questions or receiving recriminations about the unpopular war. I'd been spit on coming back to the world from Nam.

My old girlfriend was still around, but she had married just after I had returned from Viet Nam. We had broken up before my deployment. I had met the blonde surfer girl at a dance and dated heavily before my enlistment. While I was in boot camp, at a sailor-civilian riot, still just a high school kid, she had been picked off the street and hustled into a car by some swabbies, stripped and gang raped. Coming home after that I could barely talk to her any more. There was a tension that was unavoidable, and yet unspeakable. Almost every conversation ended in an argument. Soon there was nothing to say. I numbed to the rejection, and internalized the guilt I felt for what she had gone through, the guilt for being in the war, the guilt for not being home and the guilt for surviving Vietnam when so many hadn't. Even though it was gone we still corresponded.

As the anti-war sentiment grew so did my isolation. I was under orders, trapped in an unbreakable contract with Uncle Sam. I was powerless, guilty and isolated. Ride it out, I told myself.

Don't think about it too much. Just like straightening out on a big wave. One more West Pac, one more deployment and I will be free, I thought, and then it would be someone else's Navy and someone else's war.

My dad had driven me to the Goleta Airport to get a hop back to Oakland so I could join my new ship in Alameda. I wore my dress blue uniform to take advantage of a small airline discount. Navy Regulations forbid possession of civilian clothes.

The airport was full of students from the nearby University of California and I could see the hostile stares and feel their fear and contempt. It was 1969. No one, even the stewardess who spoke to the businessman in the suit beside me, and had offered him something to drink, spoke to me. After a short flight I had caught the bus to the base. At the bus terminal there had been two high school girls who had asked me and a uniformed marine how we could kill babies and burn villages? How come we hadn't gone to Canada to avoid the war? We laughed at them. Coming back from Vietnam, I had been warned not to talk to civilians or wear the uniform in public. Old ladies, they had told us, were blowing away military men in uniforms with forty-five caliber pistols.

By the time I reached the Naval Air Station at Alameda the sun had gone down and the evening fog was blowing in. I was happy because this darkness made me less visible, harder to see by the general hostile civilian population. But once inside the base I could feel the Navy closing in around me again. A marine gate guard's gruff verbal instructions had gotten me to the foot of the pier, in foggy sight of the Topa. The stiff breeze tugged at my cheeks and I faced directly into it, finding its direction. Straight west, I thought, with a little north to it. It was damp and moist, fighting its way inland off the sea and across the San Francisco Bay.

I gripped the orders in one hand, squatted down and slung the sea bag on my shoulder, steadying it there with one arm, stood up and walked down the pier toward the gray of the ship. I began to mount Topa's gangway. I ascended slowly but steadily, balancing all, hoping my white hat wouldn't come off in the chilly breeze, which increased in strength with every rung. The clanging of my measured steps on the metal ladder, the clinking of the jostled chains and the hum of the ship and the tug of the breeze were the only sounds that came to me. My hooded eyes noticed the mirthless, sullen in port quarterdeck watch, one officer, one chief and one seaman. They were all bundled well against the cold night. The young officer and the skinny chief were eyeing me.

I made it to the top of the gang plank and put my sea bag down, saluted aft and then saluted the OOD saying,

"SK3 Semmes, reporting aboard as ordered, sir."

"Will you look at those side burns! That the first thing gotta go." said the Chief in a deep southern drawl, a heavy 45 caliber pistol hung slung on a webbed belt around his waist, as he took my orders and gave them to the Lieutenant (Junior Grade).

"Boy, how long have you been on leave?" I remained at attention, as the officer logged the orders the chief circled me.

"Lieutenant, look at this mustache! It looks like a basketball team, five on each side." He chuckled at his own joke. "But no matter how small, it's gonna have to come off. The Captain, he don't like mustaches."

"It's on my ID card, Chief." I said, branding myself as a troublemaker, a mal content.

"We got ourselves another sea lawyer, sir." the chief said to the officer who stood there cold and impassioned, logging my arrival. He finally looked up and cracked a little dead serious smile.

"You won't be issued a liberty card, won't even leave the ship again until you get yourself a regulation Navy haircut, and your mustache shaved. Is that clear, sailor?" The Lieutenant (Junior Grade) said.

"The mustache is on my ID card, sir." I persisted foolishly. I was thinking again. A bad thing to do. Thinking that somehow a higher rank would see my point. There was scuttlebutt going around the fleet that if a mustache was on the ID card it could be kept.

"You don't listen, boy!" The chief was getting excited.

"Report to my stateroom tomorrow after quarters. You're on report." The officer said.

"Aye, sir." The officer turned with a tired sneer to the messenger of the watch and ordered.

"Take him to the MAA to stow his gear, get a rack." Hefting my sea bag on my shoulder, I followed the messenger down the passageway and into the superstructure of the ship, and down the narrow, almost vertical ladders into the recesses of the unfamiliar Topa. I'd been aboard a scant few minutes and already I was in trouble.

I had been left in the care of the Chief Master at Arms, a very large armed broad faced African American first class storekeeper. He showed me to Supply's quarters, advised me to pick a locker, stow what I needed, day to day, then to report back and to stow the sea bag.

The tiny crowded crew's quarters smelled. There were two hundred men, sleeping six bunks high, below the main deck aft of the super structure. The small area was divided into four compartments. The Engineering Division was on the starboard side forward and Deck Division was port side forward. They both bordered the mess decks. Supply and Operations were aft toward the heads. A dogged door separated Supply from Engineering. In the center of these four divisions lay the Ship's Store, and a TV lounge with six tightly packed chairs which were used only in port. The supply compartment had a hatch that went to the main deck. It too was only opened in port, in warm climes. The pungent reek of the urinals greeted me and I searched for a rack.

Two men, second class storekeepers that ran the cargo office, were sprawled on the deck, deeply asleep, among the piles of not stowed laundry, from a near overdose of downers and beer. A sailor crapped out on the top bunk jerked up, coming wildly awake, his muscles stiff and his body drenched in sweat. He rolled half a turn and looked down from his top bunk to the compartment deck below. I was bent over one of the tiny lockers, unloading some of my gear from my sea bag. The crow on my arm above cross keys indicated I was a third class storekeeper.

"My relief!" the man sighed. "Welcome aboard." a wildly jubilant smile of crooked teeth beaming at me. It was the first kind word I had heard aboard.

There were two heads, a line of six open toilets, three urinals and a shower room. Using one of the urinals I pissed on my good inspection shoes. The drainpipe had been disconnected. Something I had not noticed until I looked down and saw my shoes through the holes at the bottom of the urinal. The shine on the inspection shoes was ruined. I had pissed on myself.

The bunks, stacked from the deck to the overhead, six high, were strange but I couldn't figure out just what it was. Then it came to me. There were no gray Navy issue blankets on any of the empty bunks.

"That's cause they get stole aboard this ship." The sailor in the top bunk said. I was told to stow my blanket in my locker, if I could get one. The air conditioning buzzed and hummed loudly, sputtering and changing gears.

"It cain't be turned off."

"Us skivvy stackers got the black gang, the engineers pissed off."

The only bunk I could find open was one right underneath the whining air conditioner vent.

My first meal aboard the Topa was a disappointment, and a fight had broken out on the mess decks. Nobody even look up from chow as the two men grappled through the curtains and into the deck compartments.

I slept that night under my pea coat because I was unable to get a blanket. By the time I reported to the Lieutenant Junior grade, the acting supply officer, after chow and quarters, I was already coming down with a severe head cold. I had been restricted to the ship until I got a haircut, shaved the sideburns and the mustache. I tried to shave up my side burns but it wasn't good enough. I met one of the officer's stewards, a striker named Aqui, who gave me a regulation haircut for a few bucks. But I was angry and wild enough from leave and the surf to try to fight for my mustache.

I stood, at attention, dressed in blue work dungarees. My white hat folded in my hand, in front of the Lt.jg. in the small stateroom in unfamiliar officer's country, one deck above the main deck, and listened to him talk. He was a young man, about my own age, perhaps two or three years older, with a college education. He had been made a gentleman and an officer by an act of congress.

That morning during chow the officer had already talked to the Captain about the new man aboard.

"You have to break him to the ship quickly. We don't have a lot of time to integrate him. We'll run him through a mast. You, as acting division officer, can bring him up on charges. If he won't tow the line, three days bread and water with the jar heads on the base ought to bring him around, don't you think?"

"Aye, Aye, sir." The Ltjg said to the captain, smiling, showing his straight teeth. Any suggestion by a superior officer was tantamount to an order. The Lieutenant would enjoy breaking the spirit of the new man.

The officer looked up at my mustache.

"We have more important things to do, sailor, than worry about your mustache, but never the less, I'm for you. I am for YOU learning the ways of this ship. Right now I am going to bring you up on charges before the Captain at Mast." It was then that the Master at Arms appeared at the curtained door and led us deeper and higher into forbidden Officer's Country to where I found myself in front of the captain, a four striper. On the side were the Chief I remembered from the quarterdeck the night before and the seaman of the watch. A yeoman was poised with pen and paper, had a big grin on his face. The Ltjg stood next to me and the MAA was there also. I stood, bareheaded, white hat folded properly in my hand, with my face down and looked at the deck. The Captain spoke.

"Petty officer Semmes you have been ordered to shave off your mustache last night and you have not done so."

"It is on my ID card, sir." I said defiantly.

"Yes, but it does not meet the regulations of this ship. You either shave off that mustache or go to the brig." The Captain threatened.

"What should I take to the brig, sir?" I said now looking straight ahead, bring my eyes off the deck. I straightened my back. My head came up a little. I could feel the tension and the Captain's temper flare. The Captain slammed the pencil on the podium he stood behind.

"If that is the way you want it." He paused for an instant looking at the papers. "We won't take your third class crow this time. But let this serve you as a warning. Today is Thursday." The Captain said out loud in a commanding voice. The ship's yeoman began writing the sentence.

"Three days bread and water, in the base brig. We'll give him to the United States Marine Corp until Sunday. Mast dismissed." And with that he turned to go, but he paused and turned back to me.

"Sailor, you will trim up that mustache or face another three days in the brig. Do you understand?"

"Aye sir." was all I could get out of my mouth. I had won. I could keep some remnant of my mustache. I didn't have to cut it off, I only had to trim it to the Topa's regulations. Somehow it didn't feel like a victory. With the Captain gone the atmosphere relaxed somewhat between the chief and the Ltjg. The rest of us remained tense. The Ltjg gave me a big 'I warned you grin'. The yeoman gave me a surreptitious head nod, and a little smile. The MAA shackled me at the wrists and took me off the ship and over to the brig on the base run by the US Marine Corps. The only thing the Marines hated worse than brig duty were the sailors who were in the brig.

I took nothing to the brig except keys and they were taken away from me when the MAA had checked me into the facility. After about fifteen minutes in the tiny cell of solitary confinement, three shaved headed, muscled up, khaki uniformed marines appeared at the door.

"Are you one of them hippie communists?" They asked me rhetorically. "We don't like your hippie mustache, boy." One of them opened the door stood by it and the other two walked into the cell. They began yelling and screaming at me to stand at attention, which I did. The first blow was to my stomach, and I doubled over, windless. The next blow knocked me to the deck of the cell. After a flurry of kicks to the legs and back they stopped. I could hear them grunting as they forced me again to my feet. The two marines took turns bouncing me off the bulkheads of the little cell, slamming punches into me, working me over, with blows to the body and kicks to the legs. They laughed, having a great time. All I could do was cover up, and roll into the fetal position. Protect my head. Finally the punching and kicking stopped. The marines were breathing a little harder now. They had had their work out. I did not move.

"We'll be back. We got the week end duty." They said gleefully. "Next time it'll be my turn." said the marine at the door, his voice full of anticipation. After several minutes I tried to move off the cold brig deck. I crawled, little by little across the deck and over to the simple Spartan bunk and finally eased into it. There I rested and waited for the next beating. Ride it out, I told myself, just straightening out on a big wave. That was all it was. The Marines came back, every hour at first then every two hours. I took the beatings. They left me alone after his meals of piss and punk, white bread and water. They didn't want to get puked on. Every fourth meal some butter was spread on the white bread. I tried this fare and puked. The marines came in and beat me up because I puked on their deck. After they'd pushed my face in it, they made me clean it up. They stood over me as I worked on my knees.

I felt no hate toward the marines. My half-brother was a marine, joined to spite our career navy father. It happened in Navy families. One of my best friends from school was a marine. This friend's mother had been a marine during WWII, a BAM, a broad assed marine. The last time I had seen him was a chance meeting on a Grey Hound bus. I was riding the dog home to Oxnard and the bus had stopped at Oceanside, where a bunch of jar heads got on. One of them was my friend. He sat down next to me. We were both in uniform. We talked. It seems that during boot camp his mom had sent him a photo of her, in her marine BAM uniform, with a nice stand up frame, to place by his bunk. He said he took so much guff for that it was incredible. Even now thinking about it,

I tried not to laugh. It hurt too much. But I couldn't stop giggling through the pain. I didn't hate the marines. Marines had been the only thing between us and the communists in Nam. I had got them ammo, loaded them into helicopters and stacked their dead bodies at Hue during Tet '68. It was stateside that they were a problem.

Three days later, on Sunday morning the Topa's MAA took me back to the ship. I could barely walk but there were no marks visible on my face, except above the right eye, where I had 'fallen' against the bulkhead. Tripped his own self, the jar head sergeant had said.

Once back in the Supply compartment, I went directly to my locker, got my shaving kit and then went to the head. There, with a trembling hand, I trimmed the side of my mustache so it would not protrude beyond the imaginary line that went from the corner of the eye to the corner of the mouth. I used the razor to make sure that the mustache was no wider that half the distance from the base of the nose to the top of the upper lip. I carefully checked it out to make sure that it was no longer than three eights of an inch in any one place. It wasn't much of a mustache, but I still had it. I reported to the MAA, to show him I had complied with the Captain's mustache regulation order. The black MAA talked to me.

"See here." He pointed to a swatch of black hair he had growing on his lower lip of his broad face. "This is my black power mark." He said with a broad grin on his face. "When they tell me to cut it off, I always do. You know, it always grows back."

I found my rack and crapped out the rest of that Sunday. It seemed a lot softer. I had even gotten a gray woolen blanket. Evening chow that Sunday tasted good, and when a loud argument broke into fist a cuffs on the mess decks, I didn't even look up from my chow. Monday I would be getting my new assignment. I already knew what it was. The sailor on from the top bunk had told me. I was taking over cargo hold number four.

CHAPTER 2

Make All Preparations for Getting Underway!

A few weeks later, the ship was ready to shove off and I knew the names of some of my shipmates. I had taken over the top bunk along the bulkhead of the Supply department and had finished loading hold number four. The top bunk sailor, Elliot, before packing his sea bag and leaving the ship for home on the East Coast had showed me what he could of the hold. The diagrams of where the different items lay in the hold were posted on the hold stanchions on each tier level. I got a roster of the men in my hatch team. I knew few of them.

I began to warm to the Topa as home and feeder. I began standing in port quarterdeck watches as Petty Officer of the Watch. There was no surf near that I knew of, close, warm and accessible, like there had been in San Diego, so I stood watches for the married guys who would be leaving wives and kids for the West Pac Deployment. There was an exception one weekend.

The ship was shoving off soon, so I made only one trip back home. And that was to bring up my surfboard. I planned to get some waves overseas. I had surfed in Da Nang. I rode the bus for thirteen hours on Friday night in my uniform, put my surfboard in a cloth bag and then drove my van back to Alameda. With a line over the side up near the bow, and the help of Heavy, who had the watch, I got my surfboard aboard. Heavy threw me a line, which I tied to the board bag. Heavy carefully hauled the board to the main deck. I came on board and took custody of the stick. Heavy went back to standing the in port Quarterdeck watch. I walked the surfboard to the super structure, down the decks to hatch number four, unseen. I took off one of the hatch boards and slipped the board into the hold, where I hid it among the shoring.

Then I drove the van back down to Ventura and took the Grey Dog back up to Alameda. This time I'd brought one change of civilian clothes in a little brown paper bag.

Other than that important and illegal foray outside the ship's 200 mile travel limit I welded myself to the ship. I spent my free time on the fantail. From there on clear nights I could see the lights of San Francisco, and it was breathtakingly beautiful. I kept the mustache neatly trimmed.

My defiance of the Captain's mustache regulations, short lived as it was, and going to the brig for three days had been reported by the yeoman to the crew and had earned me some respect. Standing all the night watches for the married guys helped introduce me around.

I liked the cold night watches. They were lonely, just me and the messenger. I liked this time spent alone, or all most alone with the gray ship Topa. The Officer of the Deck was usually only present at the beginning and end of the watches. To relieve or be relieved. Occasionally the officers would check the Quarterdeck, to make sure the enlisted men on watch with them weren't smoking or asleep. Mostly the officers cat napped warmly in their staterooms on the O-2 level, decks above the main deck, secure in the fact that if something happened, they would be notified.

The last night in port before the ship pulled out for Asia, I stood the midnight to four for Reyes, a Third Class Ship fitter, who worked aft in the ship's repair shop. The pre watch rest was fitful. About medium height and weighting less than one hundred and fifty pounds, I fit nicely into the little aluminum frame bunk that stood hooked to the bulkhead and chained to the overhead. That is if I didn't move. My feet did not protrude beyond the aluminum limits of the berthing space, except when I stretched straight. Then my feet I could feel the frame and my head pressed against the boundary of my sleeping space. When I lay on my back my shoulders rubbed the coldness of the aluminum. On my side, when I curled up slightly, my knees and back braced against the metal side rims.

Still my rack was the prized top bunk, the highest one of six. Nobody could puke on me from its lofty position. Officers were reluctant to climb so high during inspections. I had privacy because nobody could look down into my sleeping space, and it was difficult to see up into it. I could not sit up in my bunk, nobody could do that, but because I was the top bunk, up near where the ship's steel beams crossed, there was a little space, a corner, where a book could be hidden, which could not be seen from the deck below. The officers and chiefs didn't like the enlisted men reading anything not related to professional advancement in the U.S. Navy. Books and magazines had to be kept out of sight and hidden. I had a paperback book about Indians hidden among the steel cross beams now. Reyes had given it to me. I had inherited the top bunk from Elliot, the man who I relieved. The transfer of possession had been swift and public. I wanted there to be no mistake who owned the bunk. There had been plenty of envious eyeing. There had been questions from those down below and suggestions.

"You ain't one of those guys who gets drunk and then comes back in sick and pukes down on his shipmates are you?" The Bear had asked.

"Or somebody who gets seasick." Said Heavy from another tier down.

"If you are why don't you just give me that rack now?" Bear put his rough unshaved face into mine, bluffing.

I assured them that I was not one of those guys, and had taken over the top bunk swiftly, changing the small pillowcase, the fart sack, leaving the blanket on the bunk and hanging some dungaree pants from the bunk chains. I'd also cinched the thing tight.

That night before the Topa shoved off for its last WEST PAC I lay on my left side, facing the gray steel bulkhead that was just inches from my face. Instinct made me come awake at 2330. I changed my position, one hundred and eighty degrees, to face outward with a series of little moves, placing my feet on the aluminum frames, sliding my back, then rolling up on my other shoulder. I had done it almost silently and faced toward the center of the compartment.

I looked down through the bunk chain links and listened for the messenger of the watch, who at any minute would come wandering into to the Supply Compartment to find me.

Because of my movement, even ever so slight and calculated as it had been, Bear, the giant footed, half Indian Oregon logger who slept in number five bunk stirred beneath his woolen blanket and edged his large sprawling form tighter into a massive oblong ball. The whole tree of bunks shivered with the Bear's movement. The Bear farted.

The Bear moved to his side and his hipbone brushed the bottom of my rack. We could not both lay on our sides, or hips would touch. When Bear shifted from side to back, I could lay in either side or back position. When Bear curled up on his side, I could only lay on my back. Even so, now Bear's hip was in my back. My weight pressed down on Bear's hip. It was time, I thought, to re cinch the bunk tight again. It was sagging too much. At least the only thing above me was cold steel. I was not caught between two bodies like every one below me, except for the bottom bunk, who had five sleeping above him. They were positioned alternately head to toe, head to toe.

I didn't have the only top bunk. There was four more along the bulkhead forward. Twenty-four men slept, their bunks hung on chains on the mental bulkhead. Toward the center of the compartment there were other bunks, two rows, chained from the deck to the overhead, secured on steel poles. Against the far bulkhead there was a row of tiny lockers.

I listened to the hum of the ship and the whirl of the air con. I couldn't help but think. I, Steven Decatur Semmes was just twenty-two, the time when most young men were beginning careers. I was trying to escape one. I'd been born at the Navy Base at Norfolk, Virginia, to a career Chief Boatswain's mate and named after a naval hero. I had grown up a military brat on various shore stations while my father had been with the fleet making the Europe and Asia safe for democracy and capitalism. Before I ever went to school, I could find on the map where my father's ship or station was overseas. The Korean peninsula, the boot of Italy, or the island of Formosa came to mind.

Although only in the Navy coming up on a mere four years, I could hardly remember a time when I had not been in the Navy. I had known the ranks and ship and aircraft types by sight as a child. I'd wore Navy regulation skivvies, socks and dungarees since the time I could fit into the littlest size the Navy Small Stores offered. I had used Naval issue pens to do my homework and had eaten off white mess hall dishes with Navy stainless steel silver ware and drank out of regulations heavy white Navy cups, slept on the sheets and pillow cases and dried off with the U.S.N. towels. The gray blankets I'd slept under as a child were the same type wool ones I slept under now. The skivvies I now wore were the same type I'd wore for years, as were the socks. The low cut, leather regulation cordovan shoes at the bottom of the bunk tree were also familiar. I had read two or three versions of the Blue Jackets Manual my father had laying around the house. When the Chief came home, the whole house stood up and saluted. That included the children.

I also was Navy issue, but now I'd had enough. I could not be openly rebellious. I knew naval discipline. "You see these hash marks and this chief's crow?" My father would say pointing to the golden Eagle on his arm and the cross anchors, "they can take them away from me any time some fresh ensign just out of college don't like the way I do things."

It stunk in the supply compartment of sweat and farts and of men sleeping too close together for too long with bad ventilation. We hung up on the bulkheads like mutant insect larvae, not quite ready to hatch, and would only do so with the sound of reveille, the shrill whistle of the boatswain's pipe. That was six hours away. I would stand the watch for four of those. From mid night to four. There was the smell of vomit on the deck from smoke stackers who had come in off the last heavy liberty before shoving off for West Pac to the coast of Vietnam and the Tonkin Gulf. The puke smell drifted up and mingled with urine smell that wafted from the nearby head. Above the hum of my ship I heard the approach of sober tentative cordovans on the deck. The messenger of the watch was coming to find me.

I came wide awake from my fitful half sleep to a king size piss hard on, which I stroked without moving a muscle so as not to alert the five that slept below me. I imagined I was putting it to Anh, the girl I had fallen in love with in Da Nang, and made love to in the Imperial Capital of Hue. I had turned in at eight o'clock, 20 hundred, navy time, to get some extra sleep, but the lights had been on until Taps at 2200 and after that the drunks and smoke stackers started coming in making racket. It was impossible for me, a light sleeper anyway, to get any.

The messenger of the watch stood in his undress blues in the middle of the compartment and looked for me. He searched for me with a puzzled look on his face. The middle watch was always the hardest to relieve for, that and the one at 0400 because the crowded compartment was darkened and the men asleep. If you weren't from that division how did anyone know where anyone else slept? The messenger looked around and I motioned to him.

"You Semmes?" He whispered.

"I'll be right there." I whispered back. The messenger sighed with a sense of relief, and then sauntered out toward where deck slept to search for his own replacement.

I crouched up on the rail of my bunk, cross-legged and bend doubled over so as not to hit my head on the steel beams, and folded the wool blanket. I then descended, hand over hand, down the taut chains that held the six racks to the overhead, like a monkey, past the five that slept below me and landed silently on the deck, my comrades not stirring.

I went over to the bulk head, the side of the ship past where the mess cooks slept and knelt on the deck in my skivvies, in the semi darkness and open my little locker, working the combination in the dimness of the compartment. I fetched my undress blue jumper, blue woolen bellbottom trousers, a clean white hat and my pea coat. I stood there in the semi darkness and put on the uniform, brushing whatever specks I could see away and trying to make myself shipshape and squared away before I went on deck to relieve the watch.

When I thought I was ready, I checked myself again with my hands. The white hat squared, the neckerchief tied right, a black square knot. I ran my hands over my face shaved clean from the night before. I buttoned the thirteen chances to say no wool bell bottomed pants. I cinched them up properly in the back. I adjusted the undress blouse. The shoes had a dull shine, but they were good enough for quarters or the middle watch in port. I checked my keys, heard the familiar jingle and felt the reassuring weight in my pea coat pocket. I checked too for my coffee cup, the dark green plastic one. It was light an easy to conceal. It was the one I used for watches and musters. Ready now, I made my way down the passage through the Engineers compartment, past the mess decks, and ascended the ladder to the main deck to relieve the gang way quarter deck watch, and put the heavy 45 caliber pistol on my hip. And watch the Topa. It was 2345, almost midnight.

Heavy, the Third Class who ran Ship's Store, had come to me when he found out that I was to stand Ship fitter Reyes's quarterdeck watch the last night in port.

"After 2400 me and Keoke wanna bring some "things" on the ship." He had told me that afternoon. By things, Heavy meant dope.

In the parking lot, around 0130, down from the ship tied up at the pier in Alameda, Keoke was drunk and loaded, and sprawled hammock-like on the deck in the back of a van. His legs were stretched out and crossed at the ankles like two big flat anchors. His large scared vise grip hands were folded neatly across his flat muscular stomach like a deceased corpse. His white hat covered his large dark face. He wasn't really asleep or comfortable in fact he was pissed, and sick. He was pissed at any haole, at any white man. His stomach churned and his head spun with the excesses of beer and dope.

Keoke could be a mean drunk if provoked and was so incredible strong that once provoked he was difficult to subdue.

Various Shore Patrols on the West Pac side of the Pacific had found this out the hard way. He was a few units from a college degree, but he could still play the beach boy pigeon speaking moke with flashes of brilliance, especially effective in front of the officers who because of his color, and size always took him for a dumb native. His long, high cheek boned Polynesian face held dark, deep hurt looking eyes. There was a touch of roundness to the face, and a hint of Asia in the eyes.

His great grandfather had come from China, and married into a sprawling Hawaiian family, and had instilled them with the Chinese love of formal school. Keoke had studied and had done well. Despite the Chinese connection and last name, Keoke's fondest historical fantasies were of killing the Haole Captain Cook. His dreams were of kicking out all the haoles, and re-establishing the kings, the Ali, in Da Islands.

One thing Keoke wanted to do was go through his four years in the navy and come out a seaman, just an E-3, and then he'd go back to school. Maybe he'd teach, teach the real history. One thing was for sure, he didn't want to be any officer puke.

Keoke, however, could work. On the deck force, where it took two men to carry one anchor link, Keoke could carry one in each hand. His moke jokes got him in trouble.

His buddy, Heavy, sat in the front and sucked the last of a little joint, then tossed the roach to the street. Now the car was clean for tomorrow when Keoke's cousin would come and take it home. The drug felt so good that Heavy just stayed there for a while, enjoying it and watching the chilly fog mistily drift on the decks of the U.S.S. Topa, obscuring her bow which pointed out toward the bay and toward Frisco and Asia.

Heavy jumped out of the driver's side and walked around to the two big double doors and flung them open. He reached in, took out a bottle of water, opened it and poured some into one hand. Then blowing his breath into the single hand full of water, splashed it all over, like a Mongol. The night chill on his wet face woke him up a little. Then he peeled off the civilian jacket and pulled the Navy blue regulation jumper off the seat and put it on in the cold misty fog. Over this he slung the pea coat and buttoned the buttons and put the collar up. Now he was almost regulation again. Heavy was from New Jersey and had a round face and small mouth that seemed too prim, like a self-righteous preacher. Above this mouth grew a scraggly light almost mouse colored mustache that was on the border of being non-regulation. The upper lip was broad, like Teddy Roosevelt's. Heavy was portly, but nowhere as near as tall or as big as Keoke or the Bear. He was called Heavy because he always had a scam going. He was a hustler, a rather slow moving but quick thinking, smart ass talking East Coast boy with a big mouth.

He slapped Keoke's big feet. He knew better than to poke him at the shoulder. Keoke jumped up, playing at being pissed.

"Kill haole." Keoke grunted then smiled and got up, dizzily.

"Yeah, yeah, yeah, kill haole, but we gotta get back to the ship."

"What for you talk like dat, bra. Keoke stay sleep."

Keoke got up anyway and Heavy checked their uniforms and then they began to roll and weave toward the ship in the distance fog.

A Shore Patrol jeep, the Navy police force, turned the corner and cruised nervously down the pier toward the Topa.

Heavy was carrying a lot of dope. He had hash, which looked like chocolate bars wrapped in tin foil in each pocket of his pea coat and ounce bags of marijuana stuffed down his pants and taped to his stomach and around his ankles. Heavy smiled, he was the supplier of the Supply Department, and other assorted individuals on the ship. Some were in Deck, Operations, or Engineering. Keep the yeoman happy. Yeomen were a great source of rumors. Make sure the cooks were treated right, they'd have some extra handouts. Don't piss off the Corpsman, hell, you'd have to take your shots again if they somehow lost your records. Heavy was a hustler, a cumshaw artist, trading this for that.

Heavy also ran a slush fund on the ship. A loan service, five for nine, ten for seventeen and twenty for twenty-nine U.S. dollars. That was where the real money was, the dope was just to keep the boys happy, from killing each other, from not going insane, from not going over the hill. He was doing the Navy a service, one that they, of course, wouldn't recognize. Heavy knew what they would do if the Shore Patrol or some chief or officer caught him. He knew the brigs. The ship's brig where cowboy novels were stacked in yellowing piles. The sailors loved to read them when doing their piss and punk for three days. But if caught, Heavy would not be going to the ship's brig or even the base brig, he would probably be going to the Portsmouth Naval prison.

Heavy and Keoke rolled down the dark pier toward the ship. Keoke wandered away from Heavy and over to the edge of the pier and lay over a big rounded bollard and began to puke. Heavy came over to help his shipmate, to steady him and to make sure he wouldn't fall in the cold waters of the east San Francisco Bay. Keoke tried to wave him on, with his massive dark hand. He knew Heavy was holding a lot of dope. Heavy refused and stayed with his shipmate, producing his white regulation handkerchief so the man could wipe his mouth, clear his nose. It was Big Keoke, standing next to little Heavy on paydays that usually made the sailors ready and willing to pay their debts.

A vehicle broke on the pier from behind them and lights from a Shore Patrol jeep rolled up alongside them.

"Any problem here?" The driver shouted to the two sailors. The four helmeted and armed naval police sat in a blue, haze gray jeep. The driver repeated the question while he played with his long black nightstick that hung from his white belt, nervously as if he was looking for a chance to use it on somebody. Another toyed with his forty-five. The others readied in the back. The racial tensions, always high in the service, had been exacerbated by the assassination of Dr. Martin Luther King Jr. just after the Tet offensive in 1968.

"No sir," Heavy said with concerned sincerity, "just taking my Samoan friend back to the ship." Just then Keoke jerked and puked again. The vomit poured from his mouth and ran down the bollard and onto the Topa's thick mooring lines.

The shore patrol, apprehensive since the words 'Samoan' had been spoken, jumped noticeably at Keoke's retching movement. There were only four of them.

"Carry on." The man sitting next to the driver commanded and then motioned him to continue their patrol. They drove down to the end of the pier passed the Topa, and the other ships, then turning around and speeding past Keoke and Heavy, on their way to somewhere else on the base, some place easier than a drunken Samoan. Their radio crackled with static in the fog.

Keoke dry puked. No more stuff came out. Heavy then took Keoke and helped him to the foot of the gangway.

"I'm no Samoan." Keoke spit, "Now you get on board, I'll be along." He waved him up the gangway.

Heavy hurriedly walked up the gangway, tip toeing so as not to swing the chains. He gave Semmes and Doaks a tight concerned smile as he approached the Quarterdeck. Heavy had called it right; the Lieutenant (Jg) wasn't going to let his ass stand in the cold wind of Frisco Bay. No sir, he was going to be warm in his comfortable stateroom, dick in hand probably. There weren't going to be any cursory searches, no feeling down of the pants or opening of the pea coat and reaching his hands underneath, brushing the teats to see what might be concealed.

Heavy gave Semmes a head nod and saluted twice coming on board and swiftly made it for the super structure.

Once in the quiet passageway he could hear the steady pace of footsteps coming down the ladder from the 0-1 level, from Officer's Country. It would be just Heavy's luck to meet the Lieutenant (Jg) in the passageway. He made it to the top of the ladder and slipped down the rung away from the main deck. One heel flip flopped against the metal and clanged loudly.

Once at the bottom of the ladder, Heavy turned slightly and looked back just in time to get a glimpse of some slippers and hated khaki colored pants standing at the top of the ladder. An officer!

"Sailor!" The Lt.jg called.

Little Heavy did not stop, nor even pause. He hurried passed the mess decks and flew down the next ladder rung, this time quietly landing on the next level still deeper in the ship, and then the next. He made it to his storeroom and silently worked the lock and slid the door opened and then closed it quickly. He locked himself inside. Every little cling and clang he made seemed like an explosion.

Now, again he listened carefully for any movement. All he heard was the murmur of the ship and his own slightly labored breathing. Would the officer follow him? It was dangerous for an officer, especially one as hated as the Ltjg to get caught below decks at night with the crew's quarters and the enlisted mess decks between them and Officer's Country. Heavy heard nothing but the ship making her noises. He slowly relaxed.

He was in the ship's gee dunk storeroom, surrounded by a wire cage. It sat in the hatch square of hold number four, two tiers below the main deck, one below the sleeping quarters.

He retreated to the last row of the storeroom and there turned on his little light. It was his little storeroom and private office and working area. The way he had it arrange against the bulkhead, he couldn't be seen by anyone. He was hidden. He reached under the shelf, on the deck and pulled out a little stool and sat down but not before he emptied his pockets and pants and took the dope off his ankles and stomach. Sitting down, he opened the pea coat and started to off load the dope from his pockets, carefully but quickly, one item at a time and then hid the packages in generic boxes of candy bars, razor and soaps. Heavy had the only set of custody keys to his storeroom. He had changed the locks himself. He felt safe locked in.

Heavy sat there for a minute and thought about toking just a little of the dope, maybe some hash but thought better of the idea. He rubbed his mustache with his index finger and thumb as if to straighten the curly hairs. It was not a conscious movement but a pensive one. He figured the officers would bring booze on the ship, maybe even some dope to. What was so different about them? It was all forbidden, which meant little to Heavy. What meant a lot to Heavy was not getting caught while making an almost honest buck. The only problem with storing the dope in here was that because he had the only keys he was the only one who could be responsible. If some dick head like the Lieutenant (JG) decided to bring the Chief Master at Arms down here with bolt cutters and search the place he was had. Forget about probable cause or search warrants. This was the navy and they could do whatever they wanted.

The idea was not to get caught, and make some cash, enough to marry Anna, the Filipina Chinese girl he had met on a special day liberty day he had enjoyed in Manila last cruise. He took her photo out of a special box and put it on a storeroom shelf in front of him.

He tried to get the lust memories into his mind. He could not get them completely out, so he went with the flow. He thought about her long, thick black, raven hair and her full sexy lips. But there is work to do, he told himself. He had to concentrate. Stow this stash.

Even as much dope as he had brought aboard wasn't going to be enough. He would have to score some in Nam, the P.I. or Hong Kong, some place where they libertied. It was a thought but he wouldn't count on it. He would have to dole it sparingly, try to make it last.

Heavy's slush fund, where he made most of his money, was as illegal as flogging yet who else would loan a sailor any money? What average sailor had a bank account? The sailor vises were clear expression of nature's needs, being happy again and free after being treated like dog and worked like a slave so long at sea. Someone had to help them out, and no one was going to unless it was Heavy. He'd provide the service and make a lot of cash.

With cash he could marry Anna.

He suddenly wondered if Keoke had made it back on board.

Keoke puked again then sat down at the foot of the gangway. Determinedly he began to mount the gang way one step at a time on his hands and knees. I stood on the top, on the main deck, hands in my pea coat and the forty-five heavy on my hip and watched Keoke make his climb.

"Doaks," I asked, "Please go get us some coffee, OK?"

"Sure, Semmes, give me your cup." I handed a green plastic cup to him and then he was gone, disappearing toward the galley.

I watched Keoke climb aboard Topa, rung by rung on the ladder. The giant Hawaiian climbed closer and closer to the main deck. Nobody was going to help him. Or hinder him for that matter. I had climbed gangways. I had climbed them on my hands and knees as a child going aboard my father's ships. My mother would be in tow and dad would be waiting at the quarterdeck to take me in his tattooed arms and then negotiate the passageways of the ship to the chief's quarters. Nobody was going to take Keoke in his arms when he made the main deck. People were going to keep out of his way, let him pass.

Doaks returned with the coffee just as Keoke, reeking of booze made it to the top of the ladder and got to his feet. He stood weaving but controlled and asked permission to board. Then he threw a salute aft and then one at me. I stood there passively and received the latter dead pan, not making a joke of Keoke's ascent. He stumbled past the quarterdeck heavily and disappeared into the gray superstructure of the ship. He stumbled passed the Ltjg and descended toward the crew's quarters.

My coffee smelt and tasted good against the damp chill of the eastern San Francisco Bay fog, but cooled quickly in the chilly wind that whipped off the water and wrinkled its face. There were no lights except the ships and some on the pier, dappling gray through the fog. There were no stars, just the blackest gray mist that hung over the ship, the bay, and the city. The fog and the wind and the gray ship humming, with the constant drone that live ships have. I thought, maybe the spirit of the ship knows she will be leaving tomorrow for another West Pac. Would it be her last one?

The Topa was an auxiliary refer ship built in Alabama in 1943 and commissioned in 1944 in Baltimore, Maryland, just up the Chesapeake from where Semmes himself had been born a few years later, at Norfolk. She was 468 feet 11 inches long, and had a beam of 63 feet. She displaced 7,770 tons, with a draft of 25'11 inches and had a top speed of sixteen knots. She was old and cruised at twelve. Full power runs, which made the ship vibrate terribly, were done at fourteen, but not for long. She was too old and slow to underway replenish the fast carriers. These ships of the line used her like a whore. They would have to break contact, stop shelling or launching planes and get serviced.

Topa had five holds: Three forward and two aft of the superstructure, which was amidships. The three forward were refer, two chill and one frozen. The two chill would be loaded in Taiwan. The two aft were dry stores.

The duty mission was underway replenishment at sea. Dangerous thankless work, which kept the fleet at sea so they could support the ground troops in a war that was already lost.

The old Topa sat in Alameda Naval Air station at the piers waiting to take her crew to the Western Pacific and Vietnam for the last time.

"I'd just as soon be overseas." I was telling Doaks. "I ain't got nothing going for me here, no girlfriend, can't surf, can't think, talk, read, everybody out there thinks I kill women and children and burn villages. I am looking forward to shoving off tomorrow, and it'll be better than Nam. What little I had before the war is all gone."

"Semmes, you starting talk like a lifer, you are a lifer."

"No way, I got my plans, I'm going back to school when I get out, kick back, surf, and collect my G.I. bill, lay some young white girls."

"Semmes, you ain't had no pussy since pussy had you." At the sounds of footsteps coming down the interior passageway of the ship, we stopped talking and squared our white hats and uniforms and put our empty coffee cups down or in our pea coat pockets. We made our faces blank, devoid of emotion for the arrival of the Officer Of The Deck.

The Lt. (jg), sleepy eyed, but pissed off and dressed in no hat and a blue bath rope over his khaki pants appeared at the end of the passageway. A blue and gold University of California scarf wrapped snugly around his neck. We didn't know what it was.

"Who just came aboard?"

"Sir?" I asked supplicating. Doaks moved behind me. I averted my eyes. It might do for a third class to ask what an officer requested, but all knew a seaman better not look at an officer too long without being ordered to do so. No one could look defiant, or smug. I had to look compliant and subservient, eyes carefully cast downward, or at least away, looking off in to neutral space, yet attentive.

There could be no direct stares. That was confrontation. That was defiance.

"Who just came aboard, I asked."

"I think it was somebody from deck, sir." I lied swiftly, then averted my eyes.

"I saw the big drunk Samoan, I mean the guy before him." I shrugged, then looked at Doaks.

"You know him?"

"No, sir." Said Doaks, then he diverted his eyes. We could not talk in front of the officer unless the officer asked us a direct question. The quarterdeck became quiet. The gusty wind whistled through some guy wires and then rattled the hand chains on the gangplank. We could not leave the officer's presence, for a piss or coffee without permission. We waited for him to leave, hoped he would leave.

The deck remained quiet. The Lt. (jg) looked around the quarterdeck then stepped out of the superstructure and came closer to me and Seaman Apprentice Doaks.

"You enlisted men," said the Lieutenant, Junior Grade, "Are the scum of society. Square away that white hat." He said gruffly to me. Then he looked me up and down, looking for something not to like. I stood at a loose Navy attention and watched indirectly as the Lt. (jg)'s hand reach out to me and unbutton the top button of my pea coat.

I felt the revulsion at the officer's touch, but remained at a loose attention. Any resistance would mean time in the brig, a bad discharge, and all the social problems the Navy said that would cause, plus the grief on one's family. I was had by the balls. I knew it and the Lt. (jg) knew it to. I thought me and Doaks could probably kill the bastard now. We could throw his body into the Frisco Bay for the few remaining sturgeons to nibble on. It was a great plan. So many people on the ship hated the Lt. (jg) it would be hard to find the real suspect. The boys in Naval Investigative Service would blame it on the watch anyway, and me and Doaks WERE the watch. There was nothing to do.

The Lt. (jg)'s hand reached inside and tugged at my undress blue jumper. He brushed his knuckles against my nipples.

"Is this a regulation jumper, Sailor?"

"Yes, sir. Navy BOOTCAMP issue, sir." I emphasized the word boot camp.

"I have never liked your attitude, Semmes." The officer leaned over and whispered in my ear. "Plus you're a nigger lover." The officer stood back up straight, but continued in a low voice. "The only thing worse than a nigger is a nigger lover." Then he continued in a louder voice.

"Don't be playing grab ass with your Afro buddy here, while on watch."

I had been numb for the whole one-sided conversation, and completely relaxed. What could I do?

"Aye, sir." The Lt. (jg)'s index finger was now poking my chest, his face so close, that I could feel and smell the officer's breath.

"Sailor, you're a disgrace to the Navy."

"Yes, Sir." I said, tiredly, accepting my lack of worth.

The Lt. (jg) now looked at Doaks who also stood at a loose Navy attention, looking somewhere off into space, looking anywhere but to the face of the officer scrutinizing him. The Lt. (jg) looked Doaks up and down again. He reached over and fingered the black kinky hair growing on Doaks head behind his ear and below the white hat.

"Boy, it's about time you got another haircut. Just because were going out to sea tomorrow doesn't mean you can slough off. You get a haircut tomorrow and report to the MAA, and then to me. I want to see it. I want white walls, boy, you understand? And Seaman Apprentice Doaks shave that piece of nigger power mark off below your lower lip."

"Yes sir." Doaks said meekly, his eyes blank without out shown emotion.

"You both are a disgrace to the Navy." The Lt. (jg) finally said then turned and left the quarterdeck, his back to us. We relaxed, letting out wind. I tiptoed to the door of the superstructure passageway just in time to see the Lt. (jg) turn and go up the ladder toward Officer's Country, then walked back to join Doaks.

"You want to go to college and be some asshole like that, Semmes?"

"Naw, it ain't like that."

"All them people with college are the same, man, lawyers, teachers, officers, all the same, man."

"The only way to fight um is to learn to read and write so they can't tell you different, it's the only way, dude."

"You crazy, man, you gonna be a lifer to, I ought to just beat your lily white ass now and be done with it."

"You could try but you wouldn't get too far."

We were pissed and bantered back and forth. But we kept it down. Then we mocked Lt. (jg) "Just checking, he couldn't check his own ass."

"Disgrace to the Navy, a bigger damn compliment the man couldn't give me, disgrace, my ass. He's a disgrace to mankind."

"Get that white hat squared away, the man comes out here bareheaded, in a bathrobe with a scarf on, and tells me to square away my hat."

"Semmes, how you think I'm going to get whitewalls tomorrow? Whitewalls, whitewalls, man, I'm black!" Doaks now pointed at his head with his index finger.

"Black, black, ain't never going to be white." He repeated it three or four times dancing around, partly to throw off the tension, partly to keep warm.

"The non-regulation undress jumper. Who would do that? A dress jumper, sure that was different, something to wear off the ship, but a tailor made undress jumper? Who would do that? It's us only needed to see lightening and hear thunder, to be an officer you gotta be able to eat with silver ware and walk a straight line."

We giggled and laughed, and chuckled at the stoop. But we kept it down. The Lt. (jg) was our boss and the immensity of the power he had over us terrified us so much we choose not to think about it.

The drunks came back to the old girl, alone, in pairs. Some young kids, smoke stacking, but most, like long lost lovers, lonely and desolate, far away from home, far away from the reservation, the ghetto or the barrio, the suburbs, the farms, in a strange time, during an unpopular war. They came back to the ship, their surrogate mother, and their home.

I looked at the Quarterdeck clock. It was 0330 and getting time to relieve the watch. I send Doaks below decks to find our reliefs and stood there on the quarterdeck and watched the gray fog float over the pier and the ship, alone. Soon it was off to Asia.

Aqui, a steward striker, had been in the Navy for six years and was still a seaman. It didn't bother him. He could make much more money here in the U.S. Navy serving the officers, as their personal servant, than he ever could in the Philippines, even with his college education. He could make even more cutting hair on the sly for extra cash. It was a buck here, a buck there. Aqui's older brother was also in the service and the money they could send home together, well, it was nice for the family. More than nice, it was their support.

Aqui and the rest of the ship stewards lived around the corner of the Supply Compartment berthing area. They were very far away from the stinking heads. They had the longest running presence on the ship, so they had better bunks, if only because they were further from the head and closer to the air con, but not too close. The operations compartment where the showers were was just around the other corner.

Aqui rolled over and looked at his watch's fluorescent dial, in the dim light of the compartment and saw that it almost 0330. It was time to get up and go up to Officer's Country and start to get the morning chow ready for them. It was a duty he shared with the others on a rotating basis.

He was in a good mood. The ship was pulling out today and that would mean that sooner or later they would pull into the

Philippines, at Subic Bay and he would get a chance to see his family in Northern Luzon and be home again. He would meet a girl and have some good times. He liked white girls too. Some were so massive with their giant breast and pale skin, but he didn't like the fact he had to pay for it too much. It was hard to score a nice looking clean white girl when you weren't too over much over five two. But there had been times. Yes, he would have good stories to tell when he was back home.

It was going to be nice and hot there and he would be getting away from this constant chill of the San Francisco Bay. He loved the States too. Aqui hoped that in his fondest dreams that he would be able to immigrate there after his twenty years in the Navy. It didn't bother him that it took so long to make rank. The only way to really make rank was to transfer to the storekeeper rate. That was open to Filipinos too. He had known a first class that had made it in less than six years, yet he was still just a seaman. That man's civilian education had been in computers, something the Navy was just starting to get interested in. Aqui's degree had been in social sciences. Something they didn't need.

Aqui rolled out of his bunk and hit the deck silently, unbuttoned his clean dungaree shirt and pants that hung on the bunk stations and got dressed. Aqui always tried to keep his uniform immaculate and well pressed and clean, all the right buttons buttoned. He had to be sharp for the officers and he liked to be clean and neat.

He wove his way down the passageway and up to the main deck and then walked the ladder up towards Officer's Country.

Any other sailor on the ship felt an apprehension about Officer's Country. The bulkheads had signs.

"THIS IS OFFICER'S COUNTRY' DO YOUR BUSINESS QUICKLY AND DEPART." But Aqui was more relaxed.

The Enlisted men were obviously not wanted there. If an enlisted man was there something was wrong. Somebody was in trouble or pleading for something special: a leave request to be signed, a special liberty, something. But for Aqui and the other Filipinos on the ship, it was their work place.

The wardroom, where the officer's lounged and ate, was a mess, from the night before. He started to clean it up. He emptied the ashtrays, paper and trash, bused the soiled coffee cups, pie plates and silver ware from the tables and took everything to wash. He wiped down the tables clean, swept down the decks, and swabbed them. The place was looking good for morning chow. When the chow was ready, one of the Filipino stewards wearing a white mess jacket would circulate through Officer's Country playing chimes and announcing that dinner was now being served in the wardroom. But that would be much later. Once Aqui was done cleaning the wardroom, and doing the dishes, he retired to the galley area to do all the prep for the cook. He worked under a sign which read, "SPEAK ENGLISH." That was because so often we talked Tagalog or Ilocano, Aqui thought. The officers feel threaten because they don't understand us.

Aqui's tiny black mustached face smiled, as he made fresh coffee for the wardroom and sat down to drink a cup in the pantry. The door swung open and Lt. (jg) sauntered with a pair of black regulation cordovan shoes. He held them out for Aqui, not saying anything.

"Yes, sir, I'll have them for you by quarters, sir." Aqui said to him with a slight accent. The Lt. (jg), having given the shoes to Aqui left for his stateroom, mumbling something. It was not a thank you. It was not a courtesy but a grunt to acknowledge the servant, who washed his clothes, shined his shoes, policed and cleaned his stateroom and prepared his food and almost every type of personal service. The officers saw them as foreign enlisted men, dark and swarthy, cooperative but untrustworthy.

Aqui was an expert on shoes. They were easy. He brushed them off and cleaned them, then applied polish with a piece of cotton dipped in incredibly hot water that he got from the hot water dispenser used for tea. He worked the polish in circular motions, softly, gently, occasionally exhaling warm moist breath on the shoe's crown. Little by little the polish and the moisture disappeared and a deep lustrous shine appeared. In a few minutes the shoes were spectacular, except for the big dent on the outside of the toe. The Lt. (jg) wasn't a good walker. In fact, he was clumsy. He had probably tripped on a deck cleat, or coming through a dog able hatch.

He didn't mind the personal service to the officers or waiting on them hand and foot. Being so neat and clean, he hated it when they made extra work by their sloppy ways. He didn't like being treated like a slave, but it was navy tradition.

He knew that during WWII, and before, American blacks had done his job. But it became politically impossible for that to continue after President Truman so the Filipinos had been recruited to do the menial work for the officers. They were treated with suspicion and disdain, not much differently than they treated other enlisted men, and similar to how they treated African Americans before WWII.

There were ways of retribution, if the treatment got out of hand. Aqui smiled and hummed a Filipino song.

Ship fitter Third Class Reyes put his hand on his wife's flat stomach and then moved it up to her ample young breasts. He fondled them for a short moment then turned her gently on her back and parted her thighs and slipped himself between her long legs and entered her. She came awake. They had been sleeping naked and had made love earlier. She got in time with the gentle circular rocking of his love making and clung to him fiercely. He buried his face in her thick blond hair, and nibbled on her neck. Their relationship had not been an easy one. No marriage in the Navy is easy. The navy attitude was that the navy didn't issue one a wife. The needs of the service came first. There was the low pay. Reyes was E-4 over two years and was pulling down some good bread. It was enough to rent a place in Alameda.

It was more than lack of money. It was the long periods of separation that played heavily on the marriage. Especially, Reyes thought, she'd be getting it regular and then he'd go to sea, and there she would be, in a big Navy town, going to school, working part time and living alone. Been getting it regular, but now cut off. Cut off for pre-deployment sea trials, cut off for six months

Western Pacific deployment. The standard joke was as a sailor was coming in the front door some marine would be leaving by the back door.

She was to be a West Pac widow. Some sailors sent their wives home to their family back where they came from. It was hard on the mothers, the kids, but it kept the family together. If the kids went back to the same place during each deployment, got to know the grandparents and the cousins, they would get a sense of home, of place. But that was expensive and as the kids got older, school became more important. So they stayed around the Navy towns and became Californians or Virginians or whatever.

Ship fitter Reyes wanted to send his wife home, back to his or her family, but she refused to go. She was young and headstrong. If she had not been so she would have not married him. She was in an Oakland junior college full time, and working part time. She didn't want to stop it now, to break it up for half a year and go home to Southern California while he was overseas. They had been married a mere seven months.

Her parents did not want her to marry a Mexican, just as his mother did not want him to marry a white girl, even if she was a Cuban. Both families gave the marriage six months.

Reyes was from an old Indian Mexican family, Chicanos, and he had grown up in one of the barrios of Los Angeles sprawling suburbs. Alison's family was puro Cubano, heavy Spanish blood, hence the blonde hair. They had met in high school. Reyes was a senior, good looking, wiry, tough, and smart. He had graduated from high school, by no means an easy fete in the barrio, where there was so much trouble to get into. There was so much grifa, and other drogas, and little hainas just waiting to get pregnant. There were plenty of cheapo labor jobs, so a guy could just think he was doing all right. He would be bring a few dollars home to La Familia, a few dollars to fix up the short, to get a six pack, to cruise and to throw chingasos if blows were needed to be thrown. Reyes had gotten in to welding, attended the junior college and was working toward a welder's certificate. When Vietnam heated up, he joined the Navy.

Alison had been younger, a sophomore, but they had still dated and she waited for him through boot camp, and several West Pac cruises. They had written letters. He had gone home every chance he got. Every leave and as many weekends as possible he had made the long drive down 101 from the Bay area to L.A. After her graduation and he had returned from the last West Pac, she had left home to run away with him, and gotten married.

He had not obtained permission from his commanding officer. There had been no time. That came after the marriage. He had been in trouble, almost losing his crow. He took her to Alameda where they rented an apartment in the third story of an old creaky Victorian style house. It had one room with a jury rig kitchen and head.

As he moved inside her he could not help having reservations about her staying in Alameda. Yet there were a lot of dangers for her in the barrios of the south. Either way he was shipping out. She was staying. If he had grown up in one of the barrios near Long Beach, or San Diego seeing a lot of swabs, sometimes fighting them, he probably would have joined the Army, but his turf had been on the northern rim of mountains surrounding L.A. The squids had been few. The navy had seemed romantic.

He liked his work as a ship fitter and had made third class in the fleet. He couldn't wait to get out of the Navy, get his welding certificate and open his own body and fender shop in the barrio. His young wife was for this only if he opened it away from the L.A. barrio. She didn't like the violence and the constant danger, and having traveled, she liked it. She hated it when Reyes was away. Alison wanted an education, respect and a life somewhere away from L.A.

She was going to wait in the little apartment they had in Alameda until the ship came back home. She wanted to study and work. He didn't want her to be a West Pac widow, alone and vulnerable in a town full of sailors. It would have been bad enough to be in the barrio again, at least there was family there. She was adamant and would not go south. She'd had a taste of independence and would not crawl back home when things got tough.

Then he thought of nothing else but saying his last good byes, of loving her on the last night. He grabbed her buttocks and thrust himself as deeply in her as her could. As they climaxed together in one last tight clinch and sigh, the alarm rang off the nightstand. It was time to release her, to leave her, to hit the deck, and get ready to report back to the Topa.

CHAPTER 3

Trans Pac

Under gray over cast skies, a small crowd of people, mostly dependents waited on the pier to watch their loved ones leave. They were a mixed bunch. Young navy wives with small children, tearful, tried to force their kids to wave good bye to daddy. They held kids too young to realize that daddy wasn't coming home that night, or for many more. There were older navy wives who tried to show no emotion, wore sunglasses and waved good bye with white handkerchiefs, because they could be seen from so far away. There were a few young wives without children and some girlfriends who were dressed provocatively, trying to show their young men what they would be missing. Fewer parents, but some, stood by as the ship made her final preparations. They remembered WWII or Korea.

For a ship's compliment of two hundred men and twenty some officers, it was not a large crowd. Most had visited the ship before being politely asked to leave as final preparation to get under way was announced over the PA system. There were final hugs and kisses and embraces and then they, single file, walked off the gangway of the ship and stood and watched the ship disengage herself. All water and communication lines were disconnected. The gangway was rolled next to the ship and then secured to her side.

Second Class Storekeeper Bird's wife was young and rotund, like a little ball full of jelly, jingling as she walked off the gangway slowly. Reyes's lady was stunning in red. Her long well-formed legs protruding below the short red skirt. Her ample breast filled the sleeveless black blouse. Her long blonde hair flowed in the chilly wind.

A line handling party came to cast off lines for the Topa. On the pier a bored Navy Band played "Anchors Away" awkwardly and without enthusiasm. Their eyes wondered over the dependents. The band couldn't wait to get out of the wind and back to the warm barracks. It was cold standing on the pier. The line handling party was the first to leave the pier although some hung around for a while to gawk at Alison and some of the other young women.

The ship was freed and began to take up her lines as she shoved off and pulled out. The water between the ship and pier turned a dark muddy color as the ship's screws churned up the muck from the bottom of the San Francisco Bay.

The good byes had been said, the final instructions to wives and children had been laid down. The men not on watch or doing the ship's work, manned the rails for one last look at their loved ones and home port. The married men like Reyes and Bird, and guys leaving girlfriends were in a foul sad mood. Reyes had refused to show any feelings the entire morning. Even in the last few minutes before the visitors were asked to leave the ship he was stern and emotionless, saying that they had said their goodbye last night. Alison hung by his side her arm entwined in his and they talked. They had been away from each other before, but then she had lived at home. And even after the marriage they had been separated but only for a few weeks while the ship took a pre deployment shakedown cruise. This would be a lot longer. This would be a West Pac deployment. This would be different. The other men left those with loved ones alone. They stayed out of their foul way. Anger was high and tempers short.

I watched the tearful farewells, the hand holding, the last kisses and hugs and remembered my childhood, when my father would leave. I remembered the pain. I remembered well when I had first gone to Nam years before: The knotted up sensation in one's chest when one was leaving a loved one. There was the uncontrolled hopeless and helpless remorse of doing one's duty.

This departure, this shoving off, however, was different. I had few emotional ties. I was as free as a man could be in the service, going overseas. No wife, no girlfriend and I had no chance of getting one. I was happy to be leaving the States and the hostility. Except for the communists who were trying to kill me, the Asian people treated the American sailors better than the Americans did. I thought of the women there, and of the surfboard secretly stowed in hold number four.

Topa, fueled and loaded, broke through the Golden Gate in the fog and challenged the north Pacific swells with her twelve knots. Coming back through the gate at the cruise's end sailors would superstitiously throw their white hats at the Golden Gate Bridge. Tradition had it that if the hat fell back into the water, they would go home, and never have to make another West Pac, never go to Asia again. But if the hat fell back on the deck, then they were destined for another cruise, destined for Asia again.

Once out the gate, Topa was on her own, heading west, pitching and rolling to the cross swells. She passed the Farallon Islands, white capped with guano and surrounded by millions of sea birds, and thousands barking seals. After the Farallons all visual contact with land was ended. Topa became a universe of her own, an independent command.

The Captain, the universe's all powerful god, was a tall, thin, stern man who kept to himself. His surname would be remembered, long after his face became blurred to them. He lived even above the officers, in a private cabin. He had his own personal steward to prepare his meals. He ate alone in this private cabin. In this world his orders would be obeyed. The routine of this ship, his. Reveille would be at his command. Chows, drills, watch, speed, course, and water use, would all be his to decide.

The watches on the deck and in the engine room would change every four hours. Only those involved in the changing of the deck watches would see the Captain. During the underway replenishments, he became the dominant yet distant figure on the bridge, high and away from the sailors which toiled below. There was some foggy notion that the sailors had that there was someone above him, some admiral, some government, but all these were so remote, they might as well been non-existent. At sea, on the ship, the power was his.

Sometimes on rare occasions, his unseen voice would come over the PA system.

"Now hear this. Now hear this!" Then there would be a slight pause.

"Men, this is the Captain speaking." All hands would cease doing what they were doing and listen to the man who had life and death power over them. In port all heard the comings and goings of the Captain with the ship's PA system announcements.

"USS Topa arriving."

"USS Topa departing." He was the ship. The Captain's personality, its personality. The enforcers of his wishes were the Executive Officer and the First Lieutenant, and the other officers of his wardroom.

The First Lieutenant controlled the deck and the Exec controlled everything else. The Exec was a large, quiet mostly unseen man. The First Lt. was a loud, gruff, boisterous seaman. He was a mustang officer, who had come up through the ranks. The head engineering officer was a tall, thin, spectacled Germanic. The Lt. (jg) was the acting supply officer. Directly under him were two chiefs, the pinch faced one that gave Semmes so much guff while reporting aboard and a Filipino chief whose heavily accented English was very difficult to understand.

Directly below the chiefs were Pancho and Bird, second class Storekeepers who worked in the Cargo office. They helped the chief coordinate cargo activities at sea. Semmes and his hatch team worked directly under Pancho and Bird. The hatch teams were filled with men like Heavy and Scarfi, who ran the ship's store and the pay office, and were ship stewards and mess cooks and firemen, and deck apes in the dog house.

This was the chain of command, the organization of the ship.

Before leaving the Gate, The Lt. (jg) had told the sailors mustered at the number five hold hatch square to be wary of the Northern Pacific because it was some of the roughest ocean in the world.

He should have been talking to himself.

Topa pushed through the large northwest swells. The stew burners prepared a greasy pork chop meal from the ship's slop chute for the first meal at sea. The cooks on the ship were divided into two watches. One cook did four meals, then the other cook did four. The fourth meal was midnight rations sandwiches for the underway watch on the bridge who had missed chow. The cooks were both lifer second class stew burners. One Robbie, a round faced jolly guy, reminded one a little of Old Saint Nick, put out some good chows. The Mr. Jekyll was a thin austere man who bore a striking resemblance to the Captain, in age and temperament, especially from a distance. His meals were usually raw or half cooked affairs. The meals were prepared in the galley located on the main deck and then lowered to the mess decks by a dumb waiter. Bubba was one of the line cooks. He was a third class stew burner who worked the actual chow line that served the crew. He was a short very broad African American. He worked closely with Peaches, a cook striker. He was a thin white boy, with a bad complexion and a propensity for being sent mess cooking. Since he was mess cooking all the time from the deck force. He decided to strike for cook.

That first night a young black gang striker had eaten hearty. The sea air increases the appetite. He came to regret it however as his stomach began to erupt with the new rolling of the ship as Topa charged course. He jerked up from his rack, hitting his head, then rolled out, but was held back an instant by the pitch and roll of the ship. He ran toward the heads at the end of the Supply compartment, holding his stomach. He reached the dogged hatch that separated the compartments of Supply and Engineering and attempted to leap through. The toes of one foot caught on the bottom frame of the hatch as the deck rose with a swell.

Like an up ended football player falling into the end zone he landed on the Supply side holding his stomach with both hands. As he hit on his side a partially solid white liquid substance emerged forcefully from his mouth and nose. He slid into the puke, then both he and the puke slipped toward the far bulkhead as the ship's deck fell away. He got up on the palm of one hand, slipped down again projectile vomiting as his head slapped the wet deck, almost knocking himself out.

As he crawled, stricken, toward the far head, Heavy, Bird and Pancho jumped out of their racks and started screaming at the young fireman to return to clean up his mess. He did in between puking his guts out in the head to the audience in the nearby Supply compartment.

Bear on the fifth bunk let out gleeful cachinnations kicking his legs and shaking the whole tree with his massive feet which almost always protruded from his bunk.

From my sixth and top most bunk lair I had seen the boy fall, puke and slide through his own puke to the bulkhead but did nothing. The first night at sea, since, as a storekeeper, I stood no under way watch, I just wanted to get my sea legs back, kick back and relax, lay in my bunk in my skivvies, get use to the roll of the ship. There was the same weighing and unweighing as in surfing when one was trying to find trim. I loved being at sea.

I reached up to where the cross beams intersected and brought out the book on Indians I'd hidden there. I'd been nursing it, like a cold beer in Nam, reading bits and pieces of it when I found the time.

The pinched face chief and the Ltjg made a surprise foray into the crews quarters. The Ltjg's nose wrinkled at the smell of the quarters and the men in skivvies. As soon as I saw the khaki on the deck below, I squirreled my book away. I had been busted once with a novel in transit and had been read the riot act. I would not be caught again. The few books the crew had were hoarded and passed around to shipmates.

The Jg paused for a moment to test the tightness of the cinch of my and then Bear's bunk and told us to tighten them up. He and the chief surveyed the scene for a minute, wrinkled their noses in distaste again and retreated through engineering compartment and back to the relatively fresh air of the mess decks.

"God, it stunk in there, chief! They are a bunch of animals. Filthy animals." The Jg said to the chief who just laughed. They headed topside for some fresh air.

Once the underway watch had been set, the ship times were counted in bells. There was one bell to eight bells rung every thirty minutes. It was done in four-hour increments. Of course they were not rung after taps or before reveille. At 2200 hours four bells would be rung. At reveille at 0500 two bells would be rung. At 0530 three bells would be rung. At 0600 hours four bells would be rung. Four bells and 2200 hours were coming soon.

Everybody was getting ready for the rack. Bubba, the massive Afro-American line cook was talking to Peaches, the effeminate seaman cook striker, who had checked on the ship after Semmes and had inherited his bunk near the air con.

Some were already asleep, their bodies curled away from the over head lamps. Taps was sounded and four bells rung and the lights were put out.

The banter of the supply department centered on who would be poking Bird's wife now that he was out to sea again. Bird himself wondered about Pancho's broad. Bear wondered aloud if the wives might get an accommodation medals from some Marine battalion, or maybe the whole fleet, for support. Those awake tried to hold in laughter. The banter went on, but subsided little by little and soon the only thing that could be heard was the gentle humming of the ship to the incessant roll and pitch which like a mother, rocked them to sleep. There was an occasional creak or groan of the old ship. Occasionally the ship would pitch or roll higher or lower in response to a larger swell.

The next thing I heard was two sharp bells, the harsh shrills of the Bosun pipes in the P.A. system and the reveille call. Drop your cocks and grab your socks. The loud speakers blared throughout the enlisted men's compartments.

"NOW REVEILLE, REVEILLE. ALL HANDS HEAVE OUT AND TRICE UP! WATCH RELIEVES TO THE HEAD OF THE CHOW LINE. SWEEPERS, SWEEPERS MAN YOUR BROOMS, SWEEP DOWN ALL PASSAGEWAYS, LADDERS AND

COMPARTMENTS. NOW SWEEPERS! UNIFORMS OF THE DAY: DUNGAREES, WHITE HATS, AND BLUE JACKETS."

It was irritating but comforting to be told to get up, and tie your bunk up properly, that those soon to stand watch would get first chance at breakfast that the place had to be swept down. To be told what to wear.

The shrill and the screaming were gone and the sailors rolled out. Those not used to the bells checked their watches. It was just after 0500 hours.

After chow the crew mustered on the open main decks in dungarees, white hats and blue jackets. Supply's muster area was port side, aft of the super structure, at hatch number five, Bear's hold.

The men stood in three loose lines between the hatch square and the gunnel, sipping coffee and trying to keep warm in the wind, and waiting for the officers and chiefs to return from their meeting so to be called to attention and given the daily dope. Some chattered lightly, in whispers, about nothing and some drank quickly cooling coffee which they had brought from the mess decks in plastic cups hung when not in use, from their side along with their keys. At the approach of the Master at Arms the sailors put their cups on their key snaps or slipped into the pocket of their blue jackets. The Master at Arms stopped with his back to the sea, facing them.

They looked beyond him, at the cold gray windy skies and rolling white capped seas and waited. Always it was wait, hurry up and wait. It was cold and the men shifted here and there, to and fro on the moving decks.

Finally at the approach of the chief, the big first class, called the men of Supply to attention. The chief handed the Plan of the Day to the first class and then disappeared to his own meeting. The First class put the men at "At Ease."

The First Class Master at Arms read the P.O.D. word by word, in a halting, unsure manner. There was no beginning and no end to the sentences. The document was unintelligible.

Scarfi, the Puerto Rican Pay Clerk from San Jose, turned to me and whispered.

"They do this to humiliate and embarrass him. The officers know he can't read, so they make him do it." Occasionally the First Class would look up for a shattered moment. Nobody was paying attention.

The chief returned and wasted no time in telling them what the P.O.D. said. This verbal report was spoken in such a heavy accent that it sounded more like Malay than English. The men shifted aimlessly, at loose attention, bored, not understanding nor caring much about what was being said and unable to understand it anyway. If it was something important the word would come down through the scuttle butt grapevine before the P.O.D. After all, the document would be posted in the Supply Office anyway.

It was the Bear, from his lofty position, a head above most of the rest, who saw the Jg, the officer and a gentleman, come down the aft ladders of the super structure, from Officer's Country to the main deck. On the main deck he stumbled on a cleat and fell on the wet deck, landed on his big butt, and slid into the gunnel, with a roll of the ship.

Bear cackled like a machine gun and pointed down the deck, elbowing me.

"He was the one gave us the `be careful on the Northern Pacific it's the roughest ocean,' right?" I shook my head vehemently, biting my lip so as not to laugh, but failed to suppress a smile. We watched, with a growing number of sailors. The Jg got to his feet, and tried to wipe the grime of the salty deck off the seat of his khaki pants and his elbow, to the suppressed snickers of the Black gang engineers in front of whom he had slipped. Reyes flashed Supply a big grin and a peace sign then went serious again as he turned to face the downed officer.

The Jg got to his feet and proceeded down the deck to the mustered men of Supply. His hat was squashed down on his head, like an angry cat, whose ears were flattened out, a clear sign, that he was pissed. His clothes were rumbled now, and a discerning eye could tell what had been served for morning chow in the wardroom by closely examining the stains on his khaki shirt and tie.

The men remained at a flaccid attention as the Ltjg went over the salient points of the POD for the third time. I mostly looked over the Ltjg, the chiefs and the officer to the sea beyond, wanting to feint attention but not draw attention.

The Ltjg then made a personal inspection of the men, the MAA and the Chiefs in tow. The officer stood at the end of the line in which Bear stood.

"That man is not lined up right." The officer said. He was looking at Bear's gunboat feet. They stuck out too far for him to be lined up properly.

"Move back, sailor." Bear moved back, shuffling little by little until his toes were lined up with everybody else's. Bear stood now so far back it seemed to the Ltjg that he was in a line by himself.

"You're still not lined up right, sailor." The Ltjg and the two chiefs worked on Bear's placement for a while moving him up and back until they gave up. Then the officer noticed his shoes.

"It's about time you replaced those shoes, isn't it, sailor?"

"I got two pairs on special order, sir." The officer confirmed that this was true with the Master at Arms, who also ran the ship's small store. The officer then looked closely at the Bear's face.

"No shave." The officer said. The MAA began to write down the report.

"I just shaved, sir." The Bear said.

"That's right, sir." It was Scarfi who had spoken up. "He's got a real rough, blue beard, sir, everybody calls him, "Bear." There were subdued snickers. The officer knew the Bear, with Scarfi's help, could produce twenty, maybe thirty witnesses to prove that he had indeed shaved. The ship 's P.A. system blared.

"NOW HEAR THIS, COMMENCE SHIP'S WORK."

The Ltjg was finished with the personnel inspection, but had something else to add. He assumed his position in front of the sailors. He got our attention.

"I hope you men didn't bring any booze on board the ship." He announced to the swaying sailors. The men looked around, as if dumb founded, showing no emotion. There were no smiles, no chuckles. But Heavy had to say something. He just couldn't stay still when he felt there was an obvious needed.

"That's against Navy Regulations, Sir." He said with the smirk that only a man who had smuggled on board an incredible quantity of dope, and helped his buddy smuggle on a surfboard while on watch, could have said.

The Ltjg took two giant steps toward the enlisted man, snatched the white hat off Heavy's head and tossed it high in the air toward the gunnel where the wind caught it. The hat disappeared to the white capped tossed gray seas below.

The Ltjg stumbled back to the front of the deck muster and announced, "That hat was so frayed it ceased to be Navy regulation." Justifying his actions.

Heavy lunged at the officer, but the big black first class stepped in the way and both Pancho and Bird, close at hand, grabbed Heavy and restrained him forcefully. Heavy was yelling.

"You can't do that, you can't throw away my personal property." And then if pleading to his salutary captors, said.

"He threw away my white hat, threw it over the side." Bird and Pancho, helped by others, removed him to the rear and side of the muster. His words were lost to the wind, and the sea like his hat.

Bird and Pancho, and Scarfi were trying to protect Heavy, not the officer. There had been a time, until recently, when the punishment for hitting an officer was an immediate bad conduct or dishonorable discharge. Those who wanted out of the Navy bad enough could simply strike an officer and they were gone. There was a rash of officer strikings. The punishments were changed to the bad discharges, but after long stays at the Portsmouth Naval Prison. Enlisted men are stupid, but mostly they stopped hitting officers.

The subdued but seething crew was dismissed from quarters to "TURN TO. COMMENCE SHIPS WORK." which blared again over the PA. They went to work counting the days, months and years they had in the Navy.

Reyes popped up to me on the deck and pointed aloft aft into the gray sky and the tangled masts and booms. There was a white speck trailing the ship.

"It's an owl." Reyes said with a worried look. "A white owl."

Reyes and I stood on the deck and covered our eyes and peered up into the morning grayness. A large white owl had followed the ship out from the San Francisco Bay and into the vast Pacific. A magnificent animal ashore, a dusk and dawn hunter, the owl was dwarfed in the great western sea.

"The bird will get tired, then it will land somewhere on deck. I'll capture it, take care of it. I can keep Tecolote in the ship fitter's shack, then when we get back State side, I'll set him free."

Tecolote is Chicano for owl. "Tecolote's trapped here just like we are. It'll be symbolic for us to care for him. He can eat lots of different things. We can get things from the mess decks. I'll have Heavy talk to the JACK OF THE DUST, so we can get some raw meat."

The talk on the mess decks and in the compartment and in the holds for the next couple of days centered on owls. Owls were effective in holding down varmints on the farm, the country boys said. They were better than cats, but also killed kittens, puppies and chicks indiscriminately. They killed snakes. Reyes wouldn't bad mouth snakes and instead told stories about his aunt, a California desert reservation Indian, who had taught him a respect for snakes.

Reyes spoke proudly of his Indio blood. He would point to a little circular area between his cheek and jaw where a little facial hair would grow. "See this little piece of cheek I always have to shave. I owe it to my Spanish and German fore fathers. The big smooth part, the part I don't have to shave is the Indian part.

Reyes suggested that Tecolote, or the owl could be the new totem or clan spirit for the crew of the Topa. Just like what the sailors called their "Crow", Uncle Sam's Bald Eagle, is the totem for the whole U.S.

For the next two or three days we watched the owl follow the ship and come closer and closer to the deck. Tecolote was sometimes seen perched high in the ship's aft rigging. He looked tired and fatigued.

The long work days at sea found Reyes deep in the ship fitters shack near the fan tail, using every free moment to weld together a cage for the capture and protection of Tecolote. He knew that soon the white owl would decide to come down to the main deck and look for food. Reyes went to the JACK OF THE DUST, that enlisted man who keeps and breaks out the crew's chow and comshawed for some raw meat. The Jack of the Dust hated the Jg also. He had been forced to take on and store non regulation chow the Jg had bought for the officers from some merchant ship. During Pre Deployment Inspection the truth had come to the attention of the inspecting admiral who had reamed the Jg's ass, but after the Admiral had left the blame for the cancelled liberties because of the incident fell on the Jack of the Dust. He would be glad to help steal food for Reyes' owl.

Pancho and Bird led Bear, me and the other hatch team leaders, deep in the first hold forward, preparing it to accept the fresh vegetables the ship would receive at its first stop, Keelung, Taiwan. We descended the narrow rung ladder to the bottom of the hold and worked there until noon chow as the Topa pitched and rolled through the swells.

Keoke was busy with the Deck force, first division, chipping paint with hammers and chisels. The Giant Hawaiian kept an eye on Tecolote when Reyes was aft in the ship fitters shack welding his cage. The racket of fifteen hammers on the metal deck were enough to drive a man to drink as the deck apes did after they knocked off ships work. The gang was Big Red's, a young second class Bosun. He was nervous working on the main deck, right down in front of the bridge. The Captain and all the under way watch observed his work gang. The bridge lookouts reported the approach of a rainsquall to the Officer of the Deck. The word was passed to the men working on the deck. It blared over the loud speakers.

"RAIN SQUALL, 500 YARDS OFF THE STARBOARD BOW." The pace of the hammering slowed as the possibility that the ship's course and that of the violent little storm would cross. The deck apes prepared to take cover. Some would go to the Bosun's locker or the paint shack, located on the forecastle. Others would make it to the super structure where the cargo office and the galley were.

"Pick up the pace." Big Red extolled them. Keoke surreptitiously eyed Reyes's owl high above the ship and wondered if the bird would survive the storm.

"RAIN SQUAL ONE HUNDRED YARDS OFF THE STARBOARD BOW." The wind picked up on the deck. Red kept the men working.

RAIN SQUAL EMINENT, ON DECK, TAKE COVER."

"O.k. boys, secure!" Big red yelled as the first drops of windblown rain pelted them.

"Head for the boatswain's locker." The deck gang stopped pounding the rust spots on the deck, stood up and jogged along the deck forward toward the forecastle and took cover under the eves there. Keoke looked skyward as the rain and gale whipped and flailed the ship. He saw no sign of the bird.

After the squall had run its course, and the wind had calmed and only the big drops of drain water dripped from the eves of the Bosun's locker, Big Red ordered the apes back on the deck. The pounding and scrapping started again. The sky cleared and Keoke saw the owl, high above the deck, fluttering its little white wings.

That afternoon the magnificent owl got close enough to the deck to be captured. He had descended little by little getting closer and closer to the gray super structure of the ship. He flapped his wings frantically, trying to hover against the sea winds sweeping over the decks.

Tecolote was heading for a landfall in Officer's Country. When the bird's landing seemed close, Keoke acted.

"Hey Boats, can I make a head call, take a piss break?" He asked Big Red.

"Shove off." The Boatswain mate told him. Keoke retreated aft to the ship fitters shack to advise Reyes. The ship fitter came on deck for a look see and decided to that it was time to act as Tecolote hovered a scant distant off the 0-1 level of Officer's Country. He ran back down to the ship fitters shack to get the owl cage and hood. Reyes came back on the main deck and ran toward the super structure and the 0-1 level, looking frantically for the white bird, looking for what he considered the crew's totem.

He saw the Ltjg standing on the 0-1 level with a small bloody baseball bat in his hands. Tecolote's little white feathers swirled around the deck and the railing for an instant and then were whisked away by the stiff sea wind. The officer quickly and summarily kicked Tecolote's body over the side and into the Pacific.

Reyes was furious, but powerless to do anything about his rage.

He took the white bird following the ship and its gruesome death as a bad omen. The Ltjg had killed the crew's sacred totem. In rage he went back to the ship fitters shop and gathered the gear he's been making and deep sixed it all, flinging it over the side.

"This cruise didn't begin well and it will not end well." He told Keoke, Heavy, and me, when we met in the stripped gun tub aft, above the ship fitters shack, after evening chow for a bull session and a joint. His distant mystical look sent shivers up our spines.

"NOW HEAR THIS, NOW HEAR THIS!" The squawk box blared the next day. There was a static cackle, as the microphone was passed to the captain's hands.

"THIS IS THE CAPTAIN SPEAKING." All hands stopped ship's worked and listened to the commanding unseen voice that filled the ship. "THE CREW HAS BEEN USING TOO MUCH WATER. WATER HOURS WILL BEGIN TODAY AND WILL CONTINUE UNTIL FURTHER NOTICE IN ORDER TO CONSERVE WATER."

The men, working in little groups looked at each other. Pancho and Bird had just climbed out of hold number one, on their way to the cargo office and stopped at the hatch cover to listen to the Captain's announcement.

"I told you not to drink that water." Bird said to Pancho, disgustedly.

"Did you take another shower?" He retorted.

"ANOTHER THING, MEN. BEING OUT TO SEA IS NO REASON TO BE LAX ABOUT CLEANLINESS. I HAVE NOTICED SOME ROUGH BEARDS AND UNTRIMMED MUSTACHES. NO UNAUTHORIZED FACIAL HAIR WILL BE TOLERATED. THAT IS ALL. CARRY ON." The squawk box clicked off and the crew turned to again.

A few minutes later the word was pass for Ship Fitter Reyes to report to the bridge. Bear and I, who were feeding line down Bear's hold hatch's ladder saw the ship fitter double timing it on the main deck toward the bridge and Officer's Country, carrying a pipe wrench at port arms.

"Secure all water lines." He said to us as he trotted by, his keys jingling.

We had drawn the line from the Bosun's locker. We measured it to the length of ones out stretched arms. Each measurement was called a fathom. Since I was several inches short of six feet and Bear was several over six feet, our respective fathoms of line were of different sizes. But because my lack roughly balanced the Bear's excess, the length of line requisitioned was about right. It worked kind of like democracy.

Once the line was down in the holds we climbed down after it, down the narrow rung to the first tier of the hold. We began to cut the line into workable lengths. Every hatch's square, at every tier level, were covered by long planks of board. Hatch square covers. It took two men to remove these planks and open the hold. These long planks were removed from the center and carried outward and stacked on the edge of the holds. These stacks of long wooden planks had to be secured to assure that when the ship pitched or rolled during the underway replenishments, they would not move, come loose and fall on the men of the hatch team working below.

Bear and I spent the rest of the morning and the afternoon cutting lines, measuring and getting ready to splice the line back on themselves with marlinespikes to make the pad eyes so the lines could be secured and hooked properly.

Coming on deck at the end of the day we heard the PA system call.

"Ship fitter Third Class Reyes, report to the bridge, on the double." Reyes was seen jogging along the main deck and scurrying up the ladders of Officer's Country again to the bridge and then jogging back aft to the ship fitter's shack then going toward the bridge again. This last time he went by he was again lugging his big pipe wrench at port arms. He was chugging and sweating but smiling a secret little smile. Later he explained at evening chow.

Four of us, Heavy, the Bear and Reyes and me, crowded our flat, metal compartmentalized chow trays on to one of the tiny single stanchion mess deck table and began to talk and banter noisily. The four trays just fit on the little platform table. We held arms to our sides, hunched over our trays and shoveled the food toward our moving mouths. The only individuality was how the food was arranged in the tiny compartments, where the cups were placed, which hand a man ate with. We talked between hurried gulps but the noise of the conversation only stayed among us four hunched, over our chow. Its sound were overwhelmed by the crowded busy mess decks, where every table was full and more men waited and moved noisily down the serving line. Nearby was the clanging and clattering noise of the scullery that occasionally pierced the loud drone of the crew's conversation.

"They passed the word to secure all water lines, so I did." Reyes was saying." I secured them all including the Captain's stateroom, drinking fountain and private head. The Captain found out when he took a dump that wouldn't flush. I was called back to the Bridge and got my ass chewed. And I had to open them." We all laughed.

"They said all water lines. Hell, I thought they meant it. Man that place stunk."

Reyes smiled, but it was the hurt smile of someone who had been cheated by one more powerful. We all laughed the laugh of secret revenge, the laugh of the powerless. Reyes's little revenge had been to cut off the Captain's water for a short time, to inconvenience him. The officers and Captain would still have water. That night after they knocked off from ship's work, the crew, however would shower under the new water hour restrictions.

A little while after chow, the Operations Division was the first to be called for water hours. They were directed by the higher petty officers from Engineering, armed with wrenches and wristwatches that had second hands. Naked sailors having only soap and a safety razor were allowed into the shower until one stood under the available showerheads. Their white towels were hung outside.

Sailors in other divisions stood around their own compartments and waited in various stages of nakedness. Some went to suck water from a drinking spigot next to the Heavy's Ship's Geedunk store.

After Operations, Engineering went next, then Deck. Finally it was Supply's turn.

"This is what happens when you sailors drink too much water." Bird scolded us. He had his towel around his thin waist, soap on a rope around his neck and his razor, holding it as one would a weapon, clenched in one hand.

"If you want to remain a virgin," Pancho kidded Peaches, "You better not drop your soap."

Naked, we crowded into the room and stood beneath one of the showerheads. One petty officer from engineering, Reyes's boss looked at his watch, then motioned to the other one to turn on the water. The liquid trickled out and the storekeepers got themselves as wet as possible and then started to soap down.

I quickly ran my wet soapy hands over my crotch, inside the cheeks of my butt and over my feet, then I rubbed my armpits and neck, face and ears with the water. After some seconds the water stopped. I used this time to semi soap my face and then run the razor over it, shaving my cheeks and jaw by feel. I shaved it all once then going over it with the other hand to feel for any missed spots. When the water came on again, I was ready to use all the time and the water to rinse vigorously.

The crowded bodies had been working furiously to wet and scrub down were now working on rinsing themselves. Many tattoos flashed around the little crowded shower room.

There was "SWEET" under one breast and "SOUR" under the other. Linked chains circled around wrists or ankles, with black balls trailing on the calf, signifying that lives were controlled. Above the butt, right along the waistline, one read "BEWARE OF SCREWS." It aped the warning sign on the fantail of every ship, but had darker, more personal implications. "JESUS" was big and bold on one shoulder blade. "SAVES!" was on the other. "MOTHER" and a fading red rose on the arm, a large Uncle Sam Eagle on the other. There were skull and cross bones, and the words "FUCK IT."

The water stopped. Seconds had passed. The men of Supply caught the last drops of water hours and then single filed back to their compartment. There would be another round of water for those standing watch, but if you missed that you were out of luck.

The closed in, below decks, badly ventilated and crowded crews quarters now reeked even worse than they normally did. Each compartment area developed its own particular odor.

Engineering was especially foul. Standing watches in 140 degrees heat the black gang developed an oily smell and oil stains on their bodies and dungarees, and crotch rot which could never be gotten rid of even washing in Borax soap. They did however rig a coffee can from the boiler feed pump to collect water for illicit showers in the engine room.

Deck had its own smell, that of paint and rust. For each sailor his home compartment smelled fine, the others reeked. Supply compartment smelled just like home to me. Engineers felt that Supply and Deck were particularly loathsome, and Deck thought the same about Engineering and Supply. Everybody agreed Operations smelled like a whorehouse.

Up in Officer's Country, in the super structure of the ship above the main deck, the Ltjg finished a nice hot shower and opened up the stateroom's porthole and a fresh sea breeze circulated.

Below the main deck aft, in the crews quarters the men too were drying off and putting their head kits away in their little lockers. Nobody had any doubt that the officers were not on water hours. The men worried about water being further rationed. Time reduced, or cut off all together. They worried about drinking water.

Even if those were cut, there would be enough for coffee and chow, to keep them going.

After Water Hours, Reyes and I met Heavy at the wire mesh door of the Ship's Geedunk Storeroom, two levels below the main deck.

After shower hours, those sailors who had no duty would gather to socialize. The small contingent of Hawaiians would meet together talking the pigeon. The Filipinos, the African Americans, the Okies, all relaxed, talked the home boy talk and listened to some of their music, smoked some dope, drank some booze. They met in their private areas, between the rows of bunks, on the hatch squares under the booms, on the decks, wherever they could congregate and feel safe.

Heavy looked around and listened carefully then took the keys off his dungarees and finding the right one quickly, inserted it and freed the padlock. He slid the wire mesh door open as quietly as possible and motioned Reyes and I in. Once inside he slid the door back into place and locked us in.

The caged storeroom was filled with shelves of soap and tooth paste and brushes, shaving gear, deodorant, envelopes and writing tablets, candy bars, cokes and other assorted geedunk. The storeroom sat in the corner of the hatch's square, just down from the central supply office. He had arranged it so the long rows were blocked from view from the entry passageway. He led us to the last row where he maintained records and little informal office area. He turned on a small jury rig nightlight and proffered us little squat stools and we sat while Heavy retrieved his smoking gear.

He pulled pieces of a long calumet out of one of the boxes and assembled it. There were three long colored wooden pieces and a little brass smoking bowl at the end. He also produced some blonde Lebanese hash, broke off a piece and put it in the bowl. Reyes took out his Zippo lighter and adjusted the flame low.

Heavy held the bowl, I worked the lighter, Reyes took the hit. Nary a wisp of smoke escaped the pipe. Less escaped the lungs of the sailors, as we alternated duties. One hit a piece and we were bombed. Heavy took deodorant and sprayed it around. Reyes had learned to smoke the stuff in the Barrio. I was turned on in Vietnam. Heavy had started in college.

We had just finished a second hit when Heavy heard footsteps in the passageway. Heavy extolled us quiet with a finger over his mouth and then hastily disassembled the pipe and put it away, along with the hash. Whoever it was had come down below decks and down the passageway far enough to see Heavy's little work light shining from the storeroom.

"Heavy!" The Lieutenant (jg) voice commanded.

"What can I do for you, sir?" He said walking to the end of the aisle, around the corner and toward the door.

"What are doing in there?"

"Taking a little inventory, sir." Heavy looked at him questioningly, cocking his head. The officer walked up to the wire door and tried to force it open. Heavy took one step closer to the door.

"Is there something I can help you with, sir?"

"Why is this door locked?"

"There is a lot of valuable stuff in here, sir. I don't need people wandering in on me when I'm working, if you know what I mean, sir."

"Open this door." The officer demanded. Reyes and I who had been smiling and laughing inside now turned stone faced.

"Sorry sir. I can't do that, sir." Heavy stood his ground.

Short of wire cutters and a big hassle the officer wasn't going to get into the cage.

"Well, can you get me one of those peanut butter filled chocolate bars?" The Lieutenant asked.

"Sorry, sir. It's against Navy regulations to sell out of the storeroom, but the hours for the ship's geedunk are posted, sir." The officer walked away grumbling but without saying anything specific. We three enlisted men listened hard but heard nothing after the officer's footsteps faded down the passageway and up the ladders toward the mess deck, main deck and Officer's Country.

Heavy returned to his guests, whispering.

"Bastard treats me like a dog, day in, day out then tries to get a candy bar without even trying to comsha it." A justifiable wave of paranoia struck us.

"Let's get out of here." Heavy opened the door, letting Reyes and me out. We fled upward to the main deck, then left the superstructure near the cargo office and retreated aft toward the fantail. It had been way too close. The fresh sea air that swept over the decks at night made us feel free and safe. The stars, starting just a little above the horizon, covered us. It was the last time we smoked in Heavy's Geedunk storeroom.

Just outside the cold weather fringe of North America Topa went dead in the water. She wallowed in the ocean swells and bobbed like a rudderless cork to the whim of the wind and the currents. She turned every which way in the open sea. Scuttlebutt quickly spread through the ship that she was so badly in need of repair that she was going to be towed to Pearl Harbor, Hawaii, for repairs.

Keoke and I walked around with happy as a lark smiles on our faces. Keoke would be going home and I had a surfboard stashed in the deep recesses of hold number four.

The engineers were catching hell, and repair parties, including Reyes and Striker Doaks worked their tails off. Everybody stayed out of the Engineers way. The use of uppers when going on watch and downers when coming off watch increased for the black gang during this time.

Aqui was angry, though never showed it, because it just delayed his arrival home to the Philippines.

After twenty-four hours of bobbing aimlessly Topa got underway again. It was slow, tentative at first, but then back to normal for a twenty-six year old ship in her third war. The scuttlebutt about Hawaii faded and the Captain began to run drills. General Quarter Drills, Fire Drills, and Abandon ship drills.

The long days at sea ran from 0500 to 1800 hours, plus four hours on, eight off watch rotation for those who stood underway deck or engine room, operations watches. The drills came at any time.

Bear and I spent most of our working time together deep in the holds, splicing lines, singing outrageously together, though neither could sing well. We chattered about home. Nobody bothered us much.

There were two ways into the hatch. Cargo used one and the men used one. If the Pancho or Bird from the Cargo office wanted them, they took off the hatch cover and yell down the dark ladder rungs that fell straight down towards the bottom of the ship. If the men couldn't be reached, by voice, then Bird or Pancho would climb down the vertical rungs and continue to call them. The officers never went to these lengths to find anyone. They never went into the holds. They never came down the long rung of ladders. It looked too dangerous and in fact was if one couldn't climb up and down a vertical ladder on a rolling ship at sea. The shaft was barely large enough for one man's shoulders to squeeze through. The rungs on the dry holds were slick from years of use. The rungs on the freeze hold were covered with dripping slick ice. Below, the ladders trailed, falling a long way to the deck.

My general quarter battle station was on the bow, with the gun crew for the hand fed three inch fifties. I sat high on the bow, above the gun, and shared a scope with two first class storekeeper lifers. One was the African American Chief Master at Arms. They stood there in the cold wind that swept the bow and ran through the drills for hours.

Imaginary targets were reported and tracked. Imaginary fires were fought. Imaginary wounded treated. Imaginary damage was repaired.

Bear's GQ station was on the Bridge, a wing lookout, which he manned with a set of binoculars and reported sightings.

Reyes was in Damage Control Party Number One, along with Keoke, located forward, at hold number one, right near the paint and bosun's lockers. They would hunker down on the lee side of the gunnel until an imaginary scenario forced them into action, fighting fires and repairing damage.

The officers and crew did their normal work of getting the ship across the Pacific and preparing for our duty assignment off the coast of Vietnam. We drilled for emergencies. In the off time we congregated.

One of Keoke's regular standing duties was the fan tail watch. He stood it with a headset on and watched the trailing wake of the ship to make sure that if someone fell overboard he would be seen. The station was manned at all times. He would throw a buoy and alert the bridge. He watched the rise and fall of the swell and the albatross circle the fan tail of the ship in big figure eight's. He got high with Heavy, Reyes and me, and others, if his watch coincided with our free time.

It was a safe, windy place and if an officer did venture back the joint we were smoking could be easily tossed like a common cigarette over board. The winds whisked any funny smells.

The albatross were magnificent large gray birds with a very large wing span that allowed them to glide effortlessly on the up currents from the swells and never flap their wings. For me it was surfing air. We would watch the birds ride the winds, swooping and soaring until dark cut the view or we became too cold, then the we would go into Reyes' ship fitter shack and kick back and talk about things: Reyes' wife, my surfboard, Heavy's dad's business, Da fight for Hawaiian culture.

One early morning before reveille I came on deck to find a tropical green Island to starboard. Keoke was on the deck with his big brown eyes moist with tears, calculating the distance for a swim. He had come down from the bridge. He had been on watch.

"Semmes", Keoke said tearfully, pointing to the island and wiping his cheeks with his regulation white handkerchief, "That's looks like home. That is home."

"It's beautiful." I said. It was all green. It looked like the Hawaii I had seen from the air while going to Honolulu on R and R from Vietnam. This was much more isolated than that. Hawaii seemed the perfect place, not so cold and foggy like the coast of California and without the torrid heat of Vietnam and Asia during the blistering summers. Paradise, if one could keep from getting beat up by the local boys who never like the haole, the foreigners. The waves, warm water and the off shore winds, it was perfect.

"One more year and it's your Navy, haole." Keoke said not looking at me. Da Haole missionaries, come Hawaii, teach us to pray, to bow our heads, when we look up, all the land was theirs. Your haole brothers, they try to stop surfing too."

Keoke was hostile and pensively sad, watching the ship pass his heritage, his home. There was nothing I could do but stay silent and watch Keoke's Island slip astern.

Keoke could at least relate to a place as home, which is more than I could do. I looked around the ship. It looked as much like home as anywhere I'd been. There were some points and beach breaks in California that seemed like home. I knew that these surf spots were not home. There was no home for me. My family had moved every three years even when the orders stopped coming and my father had retired. It had become force of habit.

My home parish was not where I had been confirmed, or where I had received my First Holy Communion. My home parish was the Military Vicariate, located in New York, a place I had never been, because I had been baptized in the chapel of a U.S. Naval Station in Norfolk, Virginia. Even my religious home parish was the Navy. I was free and bound to no spot like I imagined a farmer was bound to his land, or Keoke, to his culture and his island.

A chill ran through my body even though the decks of the ship were not cold in the early morning. Could I make it on the outside? Not being told what to do, what clothes to wear or what to read or what to think. Was that freedom? A decision would come later. Until that time, Topa was home.

The ship's bells sounded, reveille was announced, and the crew was called away to chow with the watch relieves at the head of the chow line. I watched Keoke alone on deck, watching his home islands fade away aft and went below to the mess decks to line up for morning chow.

"If it ain't the damnedest thing." Bear was saying at chow. "I go up to talk to Robbie, see if them stew burners can make a shipmate something special for his birthday, only I find out it ain't my birthday. He tells we just went across the International dateline and we skipped a day. That day was my birthday!" The big man put his head down and looked at his chow.

"Don't worry, Bear." Heavy said.

"Yeah, coming back we can celebrate it twice." Reyes joined in.

"And there's probably about a zillion to one chance we'll be coming back here on exactly your "B" day, bro."

The next day we were lined up for morning chow in the mess hall having eggs to order. Bird said to Bubba, the short but massive third class cook who was head of the chow line....

"Whip it out, Bubba." Bubba zipped down his white mess trousers and pulled out the longest and biggest human penis anyone had ever seen, and laid it on the clean stainless steel border that rung the serving counter.

"How you want it, boys?"

"Over stiff, Bubba." Bird said slapping the counter with his ball cap, and cackling hideously. The other men in the front of the line joked. Peaches snickered again and someone in the back of the line said in a loud voice.

"Good morning, sir." Bubba quickly put it back in his pants turning slightly around away from the approaching officer. He came in, checked to see that all was in order and then left with only "Carry on." This meant that everybody could return to what they were doing. The officer didn't know why but people laughed. Bubba kept his thing in his pants.

Everybody was in a good mood. After weeks of work at sea, countless drills and four on and eight off, the Eagle was gonna crap today. After evening chow the mess decks were to be cleared. It was going to be payday in cash at sea.

The Ltjg came down armed with the forty-five on his waist and Scarfi, the dispersing clerk at his side. He set up a long table at the end of the mess hall near the milk dispensers, and between the dumb waiter shoot and the pea green curtains that led to the Deck compartment. On this table he placed a metal box and numerous sheaves of paper, which contained the money and how much each man was to be paid.

Scarfi and the Ltjg hated each other. The officer felt contempt for the enlisted man and sailor was embarrassed to be seated with the officer in the crew's presence.

"Can you trust that puke?" Scarfi was referring to the Ltjg. He had asked his shipmates this same question before every payday.

"Then when he gives you your money, count it out to make sure he's right. Just don't take it. You're signing that you got it. You ought to make sure it is right. How do you know he ain't shorting you and pocketing the money?" Scarfi had pointed out to them.

The men lined up in a loose alphabetical order that firmed up and quieted down the closer it got to the front. The men individually approached the table where Scarfi and the Ltjg sat. Scarfi called out the name, rank and the amount. The officer counted out the money, then plopped it on the table. The man would pick up the money, hold it in one hand and then Scarfi would show the sailor where to sign. Scarfi pleaded with his eyes for someone to count the money, but the men picked up the money and exited the mess decks through the Deck compartment, as usual.

"Semmes, SK3." Scarfi called out and I approached the table. Scarfi called the money out. The Ltjg counted it out and plopped in on the table. I picked up the money, paused for an instant and began counting. Scarfi smiled surreptitiously. The Officer scowled.

"It's short ten bucks, sir." I said emotionlessly putting the pile of money back on the table. The Officer's face turned red. He asked Scarfi to tell him again the amount, then picked up the sailor's pile and recounted it. He took an additional ten dollars from the metal box and placed on the top of my little stack of bills. This time I did not count the money. I initialed the pay sheets and fled past the curtains and into Deck's Compartment. I felt a rush. I had had the gall to count the money the navy was giving me. Next I thought I might even register to vote.

As I entered the Deck compartment, I almost bumped into the sailor who had gotten paid before me. Just inside the curtain was Heavy with his little black account book and Keoke, looking like he'd kill any haole who refused to pay. The man before me was dutifully counting out his pay to Heavy who noted it in his little book.

That night at sea there wasn't a movie.

The Ltjg retreated with the other officers to Officers Country for poker games, except for those on the watch. The crew was left below decks, their pockets brimming with cash. Heavy's slush fund waited if they ran out.

Every office available to the crew became a place for poker and every corner of the ship became a place for a crap game. The supply shack, the ship fitters shack, the cargo office. Topa became a floating gambling casino with penny ante to high stakes action.

I sat in for a while in a penny ante game in the supply office, won heavily with beginners luck, then left the game to another and went up to get a drink. The biggest crap game was right at the drinking spigot between the Supply and Engineering compartments. One couldn't get a drink.

Scarfi had the dice, and kept rolling sevens and shooting his wad.

"Shoot twenty." He said throwing a crisp bill on the deck in front of where he was kneeling. The bet was covered quickly as two fives and a ten plopped on the deck. He rolled seven but didn't touch the money.

"Shoot forty." He won again.

"Shoot eighty." Now the bets took a little longer to cover but the money was there. The people watching were making side bets on Scarfi's action below.

"Shoot one-sixty". He said hoarsely. He rolled and crapped, losing the dice and all the money. He left the game brushing past me. Scarfi was sweating profusely at his forehead and his black hair was sopped. He was smiling. He had had his fun and was leaving the game down twenty.

Doaks had the dice now, taking them and scooting into position. He rolled, with style and grace and exaggerated hand and shoulder motions and pleading expressions on his face. First he rolled an eight. Then rolled again and made the eight. He kept rolling eights and sixes and kept making them. He bet twenty, or forty each time and then squirreled some of the cash away in his shirt that had a button open at the gut. He wasn't winning big but he was always winning and chipping away. The side bets became intense.

"I got five no eight."

"You covered, man." another would say covering the bet of five or two or ten dollars or a dollar on Doaks' possibility of making his eight, or six or nine or five without rolling a seven. He was on a roll.

Aqui and some of the Filipino stewards who were in the hot fast moving game had had enough. Doaks rolled the dice off the bulk head but before they bounced back to be read, Aqui put his spit shined black regulation cordovan shoes, pinning the dice saying, "No dice." He made a cutting motion with his hands. Doaks rolled again.

"No dice." again was Aqui's call. Doaks then rolled twice without getting his number and rolled again. Aqui again stopped the dice, trying to interrupt Doaks' rhythm. Doaks failed to roll his number, crapped then lost the dice.

They looked at each other across the shoulder to shoulder crowd, Doaks to Aqui with intense hate, Aqui to Doaks with apparent nonchalance. Doaks was isolated. There were few blacks on the ship and those had little to do with the seaman apprentice. Aqui in Doaks' mind was just an officer's flunky, but there were plenty of Filipinos on the ship and they worked together.

Doaks lunged for Aqui's throat with his hands and Aqui came up with a knife under Doaks chin. Others grabbed and pulled them apart. Doaks was spun around toward the supply compartment and left the game.

Aqui grouped among his friends knew that he had made an enemy, crouched back down in to the crowd but with weary eyes and covered some of the small side bets with a couple of crisp new one dollar bills. He really didn't like to gamble. It was a social thing.

Doaks had made a little cash, but he could have made more. He circled around passed the Filipino bunks of the Supply compartment and past the shower and Operations and found his own bunk in deck. Because he was moved around so much he always got the worse bunk in any division. He'd beat his meat after taps and think of putting it to some Filipina chick when he got to the P.I. He would carry a knife too, go to the galley and get one. Sharpen into a nice short shiv.

In the light of the supply compartment, Heavy, on the fourth bunk, below Bear and me, had his little book open and was already loaning cash to the big looser compulsive gamblers. I lay in my top bunk and felt the Topa's gentle roll lift and lower the ship among the waves, reading, listening to Heavy make accounts.

I was afraid to gamble too much. I had heard the stories, had even seen some myself. The man has done his four years, his first hitch. He's ready to get out, to be discharged, but had become indebted. His creditors are waving papers in front of him on one side and the Navy is waving shipping over papers, re-enlistment papers on the other. Those re-enlistment papers come with a bonus, a bonus big enough to get his creditors off his back. So the sailor re ups. He signs over his freedom for another six years to get out of debt. I was making, as a third class over two years, what seemed to me good money, more than two hundred and forty dollars a month. It was much more than I had made in Viet Nam, even with combat pay by more than one hundred dollars. It was more money than I could spend or piss away. It was three times what it costs to rent a place in Ventura. I stashed the money away, some in the bank and some in cash. I was going to have an option, a real option, if, in fact I wanted to leave the Navy. I wasn't going to be forced into shipping over because I was in debt.

I finished reading the little paperback book and placed it in its hiding place within the metal cross beams at my head. I drifted off to sleep, with my arm over my eyes to protect them from the glaring compartment light. Soon I was deep in my favorite dream: riding glassy well shaped waves at the Ventura Point. Schools of silver smelt parted, escaping my surfboard as I trimmed along the face of the wave and down the point and into the bay.

Past taps, later that night, I awoke from a dream of a different sort. After a satchel attack on the base, we had been checking the bodies of the dead gooks, turning them over, and going through their stuff. The dead face that stared up at me was Nguyen, a kid we had working for us during the day.

In the dimly lit supply compartment, to the roll of the sea, I heard the grunts and cries of what sounded like sex. I lay deadly still and listened to the moans, then slowly semi sat up and peered down from the head end of my bunk.

Bubba's bottom bunk beside the troubled air filter ventilation system was rocking back and forth gently. Bubba was putting it to Peaches' butt and I could see one of Bubba's big hands clasping Peaches' hip bone, and moving it back and forth, their bodies locked in embrace.

I lay back down and grabbed my dick and thought of the blonde surfer girl I had dated prior to my enlistment. Then I thought of the pretty Vietnamese girl Anh I'd known in Da Nang and Hue, her black thick silky hair, almond shaped eyes framed just under the brim of a conical hat, how her petit body swelled in the wet white ao dai after a surprise shower. And other times her black silk pants and white or blue work blouse, with those white buttons I loved to undo.

Days later in the Western Pacific Topa had one the last general quarter drills before the ship reached Formosa. We were twenty-one days out bound from the Bay. Bear and I were deep in the hold finishing up the splicing of the lines that would keep the wooden hatch covers up during underway replenishment at sea, and failed to hear the GQ go down. By the time we were missed and alerted the whole crew except us, were already on station. We came up from the fifth hold of the ship aft. Bear scurried to his battle station amid ships quickly, but I had to run almost the length of the ship, past officers and damage control parties, and then up the deck before the super structure in full view of the con and the Captain and the bridge. Those in the last damage control party hovered near the boatswains sail locker just before the climb into the foc'sle, looked at me in hate and disgust. I was throwing the timing off.

After I embarrassingly climbed into my position at the gun fire control station just behind the bow gun, put on my steel pot, and had my shirt's collar buttoned and dungaree pants tucked in my socks the first class with which I shared the station reported to the bridge.

"Fire control one, is manned and ready sir." I didn't have to look around although I did, for an instant, glance toward the bridge, to feel the icy stares on my back that were coming down from the pinnacle of command.

We were kept extra, extra long at GQ stations that day. The sea wind that ran off the bow, had been cold and biting many days out from San Francisco, but now was heavy, humid and hot. I looked out on the sea and felt and saw her beauty: rolling swells, white caps and flying fish escaping from the gray ship's white bow wake. Everyone was thinking of Taiwan in a few days. I had cash to throw away.

The last night before Formosa, we were shown a training film on V.D. In the film men with syphilis had sores on their penises and there were interviews with fourth stagers who could not remember their names. Twenty- two days had been a long time at sea, then again...

The last full day out to sea, at the dispensing machine, a sailor drew some milk, tasted it then puked it and his breakfast all over the deck. The milk had curdled. We were very close to Taiwan now.

CHAPTER 4

Deployment: Western Pacific.
Keelung, Taiwan, The Republic of China

"In the Final Analysis, Reliability when deployed is the Object of all our Efforts."

I awoke before reveille and went on deck. The Topa chugged in the swells of the Keelung roads, awaiting the Chinese pilot to come aboard and direct us through the narrow port mouth and into the harbor. There was a light humid rain falling into to otherwise perfectly glassy swells.

After twenty two days at sea it was a relief to be in a liberty port. Arriving by sea one was acclimatized upon arrival. As the ship pulled closer to the Asian mainland it had slowly but surely become hotter and more humid.

It had been different, two years ago, getting off the plane in Da Nang, Republic Vietnam, dressed in woolen blues April 1967. The air, humid and heavy, had hit me in the face as I exited the aircraft. I began to sweat. It was pitch black. The Viet Cong were hitting the base with rockets and mortars. Flashes and thumps could be seen and heard and felt in the near distance. After a long wait in the dark, we rode cattle cars to transit barracks in Tien Sha. Compared to that arrival, this arrival in Chiang Kai-shek's anti Communist Island bastion, Taiwan, was positively peaceful and serene.

Keelung and the port area were surrounded by high lush green hills. It looked as if the Topa was entering a canyon. The flat areas were packed with multiple storied dwellings. The port was busy and bustling even at dawn. Merchant ships were moored everywhere and the Chinese Nationalist navy maintained a heavy presence. Old destroyers, tugs and LSTs were everywhere.

The ship's work there was limited to, first the on loading of tomatoes and other fresh vegetables and fruit for the fleet operating in the Tonkin Gulf. Secondly, she off-loaded food stuffs for the local ships and shore stations.

As soon as connections with the shore facilities had begun, the business of loading and offloading began. While most of the crew who had been standing the endless underway watches aboard the Topa were inspected and went on liberty, the cargo division got to work now. We checked the cargo that was loaded or unloaded, and supervised the stowing.

The workers were Chinese stevedores, who except for the supervisor spoke little English. They were in identical uniforms. They worked together efficiently and quietly. Almost as soon as the ship was docked a new officer reported on board the Topa. The Lt. Commander was regular navy and assumed the responsibilities of the supply officer. He became the Ltjg's boss. I first saw the commander by accident. I was checking fresh vegetables as they were being loaded into hatch number one and showing a Chinese stevedore boss a small photo of a surfer riding a wave which I had sacrilegiously cut from Surfer Magazine, and pasted in a little pocket note book. I was busy asking the Chinese where on Taiwan, near Keelung was surfing possible.

The stevedore boss had taken hold of the notebook and was studying it in the holds light as I explained the salient points. Intent on what information the conversation might bring, I had failed to see the officer climb down the rung ladder into the hold and did not hear his approach across the hatch square, above the whining of the winch motors.

Suddenly I realized that there were three people looking at the photo of the man sliding across a smooth faced wave and that one wore the khaki pants of an officer or a chief. I came to a swift but flaccid attention, putting my clipboard at my side and said.

"Good morning, sir. May I help you sir?"

"What's your name sailor?"

George Yenney

"Semmes sir. Storekeeper third class, sir.

"You a surfer, Semmes?"

"When I get the chance, sir."

The stevedore proffered the little notebook to the officer who took it and scrutinized it, then gave it back to me.

"Well, that's good, sports keep you in shape. Think there's any wave riding here in Formosa?"

"Maybe, sir."

"Should be, it's an island. Carry on." The officer gave the notebook back to me and went about his personal inspection tour, climbing out of the hold and back onto the main deck.

The next day at quarters the Ltjg introduced the us to the new supply officer, the same officer who had come into hatch square number one, the Lt. Commander.

"NOW LIBERTY CALL, LIBERTY CALL, FOR SECTIONS TWO, AND THREE TO EXPIRE ON BOARD..." The time and the date were given. The announcement continued...

"ALL MUSTACHED MEN REPORT TO THE NUMBER FOUR HATCH FOR INSPECTION BEFORE LIBERTY. The ship's work was almost finished and there would be several days of liberty for the crew in sections as the last touches on some engine room repairs were finished.

Liberty in the Navy is not a right. It is a privilege that can be revoked at any time. Sailors have been restricted to the ship for years with a device called "in port restriction." At sea the sailor was free but in port, he could not leave the ship. Out to sea for a month, and in port for a couple of days, it took a long time, sometimes years, to work off in port restrictions.

Down in the compartment, everybody was tying their neckerchiefs and shining shoes in an attempt to get past the quarter deck watch. Those who had mustaches mustered on the hatch cover to go through the Jg's inspection. Some were sent over for liberty, others were sent below for sprucing up and others were told to turn over their liberty cards until some blemish, real or otherwise were corrected.

I had my clean white hat two fingers above my brow, and my uniform was squared away. The Jg stood before me, scrutinizing a mustache that could not and did not protrude past an imaginary line that went from the corner of my thin lipped mouth to corner of my pale blue eyes. The Jg looked at a mustache that could not and was not but one half the width of the distance from the bridge of my nose to the top of the lip. This mustache could not be more nor was more than three -eighths of an inch long in any one place.

"Sailor go below and trim up that hair on your face." The Jg said to me. I started to leave the muster when out of the nowhere the Lt. Commander appeared.

"Semmes' mustache is OK". The Commander said. I remained dead pan, expressionless and motionless, as all sailors did when they were being talked about or judged by those superior. I was not in the conversation although it was about me. I stood there like a pawn, like a slave, passive and without emotion. My personal loyalty to the commander began that day.

The livid Jg looked at me. There must be something else to hold me away from liberty, a scuffed shoe, dirty whites or a white hat, no haircut, but there was nothing.

"He can go on liberty." The Lt. Commander said and walked off the deck towards Officer's Country. I hesitated a minute then joined my friends at the gang way to ask permission to leave the ship and salute the colors, the American red, white and blue that hung at the fan tail.

The less experience sailors traveled with those who knew Keelung. They traveled in groups of five or six, ten or twelve, but the groups got smaller and smaller the further they got from the ship as men dropped off here and there finding comfortable places.

It was a short walk from the ships berthing area, to the gate guarded by heavily armed Chinese marines. Outside that gate was the bustling crowded city proper.

Across the street upon leaving the base was a long line of skivvy houses and bars which served the fleet. The first place the shoal hit was one of these. We had followed a sailor that had been to Keelung on a tender. He had spent months and not just a few days in port. All the Topa men took seats around the outside of the small club's dance area and we ordered drink from the hostesses. We had unknowingly invading the regular haunt of another ship.

There was another ship's complement in the bar. It did finally dawn on us when all the hostesses moved to the far side of the room and took up defensive positions.

There was tension and hostility as both sides sized each other up. The shoal from the Topa was out-manned. One of the sailors from the other side of the room came over to the Topa's group. He stood in front of us. He had been in the bar a while drinking but was not stumble drunk.

"Your Navy sucks." The Topas agreed to that. We had no love lost for the Navy. Since this drew no response the home ported sailor tried again after looking the ship's patch on the right shoulder sleeve of the Topa's man's uniform.

"The Topa sucks." The Topa man said nothing to this. There was grumbling behind him. Maybe the Topa sucked, but only a Topa man should run her down. We bitched about the Topa, but if sailors couldn't bitch, they wouldn't be happy. Topa was our home.

The man looked to the Topa's man's other shoulder, the left one, to see his rate. He could see the cross keys which sat beneath the American eagle and above double red chevrons.

"Storekeepers suck." Stores jumped up and smacked the dude in the jaw and he flew back on his butt across the floor and the battle was joined, as we left our seats for combat. The girls shrieked and screamed moving further away. Chairs flew and glass was broken and tables turned over and men boxed, wrestled and rolled everywhere.

Pancho had seen the barkeep hit the phone and knew they were calling the shore patrol. He pulled me away and we exited the bar, throwing the last blows and pushing an assailant back toward the fray. The men of the Topa had made a mistake. We had invaded another ship's regular bar and were getting run out, little by little. It was a rout, every man for himself.

Pancho and I walked on the narrow streets. I was feeling the effects of the one drink I had guzzled down before the fight started. The streets of Taiwan were narrow and cluttered. There were plenty of other bars and other places to go. In the time we had been in the bar the sun had gone down and the artificial glitter of Prosperity Island had come on.

Pancho stopped in front of a bright multistory building fronting a traditional red and white barber's pole. Several muscled up tattooed Chinese were busy working on shoes. Beyond them there were electric sliding doors at the entrance.

"I don't need a haircut, Pancho." I said. Pancho replied in his tight, slurring Philadelphia drawl.

"You could get a haircut here, a manicure, pedicure, or your ears cleaned out but basically it's a massage place." The sliding doors slide open and a beautiful young woman in a traditional chi pao, the high collared, ankle length bodice fitting dress cut on the side to the thigh came out and talked to us. Pancho looked at me. My mouth was a gape. She was the prettiest girl I had seen since Anh in her white ao dai.

"So you think you might want one?"

I nodded.

We walked past the shoe shine stand. The door slid back and we were greeted at a front desk. Off to the side were a bevy of chi paoed dressed young women waiting for assignments. A tray of piping hot hand size face towels was offered to us. We took them and wiped down and cleaned our faces and forearms.

"Massage, gentleman, or haircut, what be your pleasure tonight?"

"Massage." We said and a lady led us down a well-lit passageway, past many rooms where I could see the chi paoed women working with their clients, cutting hair, cleaning ears, giving massage, one standing on her clients back, hands braced on the ceiling.

We were seated in two of the chairs and tea was served. Then two young women came in and started talking amongst themselves in Chinese. One introduced herself as Jade, and the other was Lily, in broken English, and went to work. They had us take off our white liberty blouses and shoes then sit down. The chairs were lowered to a prone position. Both of us were looking at the ceiling. One of the men we had seen outside came in and asked if the shoes needed shining, using hand signals. The price was discussed in pigeon and we agreed.

First, with hot towels Jade washed my face, neck and arms engaging me in simple conversation.

She went to work on the face, working the points around the eyes and the forehead. Then with additional hot towels the beautiful young woman starting working the neck muscles with her incredible strength. She worked upper neck, near the head and then the lower neck and shoulder areas. The tension began to melt away. Jade worked down the arms kneading and finding the points of pain all the way down to the fingers. The pectorals and the stomach area were next. Almost touching the genitals Jade worked the upper thigh. As she moved from one leg to the other I reached over and got out his little note book with the little photo of the surf and the surfer riding the wave and showed it to her. I asked "Where?" They both looked at the photo and then had a lengthy spirited conversation in Chinese that almost sounded like an argument.

Jade finished my front side and turned me on my back. "How you say in English?" She asked as her strong arms started searching for the tight points in my back.

"Surfing."

"Sur-fin." She repeated. "Taiwan have. Near my home place. When you go?"

"You go with me?"

"Can do. When?"

I thought about that. If too far I'd need special liberty. It would have been impossible before the arrival of Commander. Perhaps now an outside chance anyway but worth a try.

"How far? How long get there?" I asked.

"You need one day. Leave Keelung 4:45. Get Da Hsi 6:50. Come back leave Da Hsi" She thought for a moment... "maybe 12:30, get back Keelung 15 o'clock."

"O.K. I'll try to ask permission from Commander. Day after tomorrow O.K.?"

"O.K."

Arrangements were made and Pancho and I ate a bowl of noodles with the girls inside the massage place and made it back to the ship neither laid nor drunk, and with only a set of bamboo chops sticks and a plan to show for the first night's liberty. But after the massage I felt like a new man. I was thinking about the waves I might be riding.

Later that night in my little rack, I thought about the pretty Chinese girl that I was going to take surfing.

In my mind I was riding a long point break wave, the water was cold, so cold but the wave was perfect. The off shore winds whipped the white spray around my face and little oxidized salt crystals formed on my eyebrows. The waves were good size, even big. I was feeling the thrill of the drop.

The results from the fight were that only two of the Topa's men didn't escape and were picked up by the Shore Patrol. They were beaten worse by the Shore Patrol than they were by the fight, and then returned to the ship where they were restricted to the Topa for of one night.

Me and Bear worked all day with sullen but busy Chinese stevedores, who took turns eating canned fish they pilfered from the holds. I tested my skill with the chopsticks and joined them in a can of salmon. I found I could use them fairly well and after I was done washed them well and put them back in my locker.

I had the duty and wouldn't have been able to go over the next day except that Reyes, the faithful Reyes, who only went on liberties to buy consumer goods for his wife or family, stood by for me.

I had done the same thing while stationed on the repair ship in San Diego after I'd had come back from Nam. Two dollars on any night and five dollars on the week end day would get me a standby and I would either hit the beach around Dago or drive 'home' to Ventura to surf the smaller but much better formed south swells that hooked in there. Now San Diego, there was a good liberty town for me.

The next morning at quarters I ran a chit through the Chief for special day liberty the next day. The Chief disapproved, and so did the Ltjg. I was hand carrying it through Officers Country when the Commander saw me in the passageway. I presented him with the special liberty chit.

The commander asked, "Why do you want to go on this liberty? Are you going to get drunk and then sleep it off in some cheap whore house ashore?"

"No sir." I replied. "I heard there is some place to surf down the coast and found someone to take me.

"You want to surf?" The commander said and I thought that it would be denied, but the Commander loved sports.

"For sports, you bet." He said and signed the chit. I felt an incredible sense of relief and euphoria.

"Thank you sir, thank you sir."

"Now take your chit and get out of Officer's Country, and Semmes, be careful. This is the tropics, don't get too sun burnt."

The Ltjg went on liberty too. He had dinner with his brother officers. All of them dressed in civilian clothes. Then he had left them and got a taxi, giving the driver the name card of a place that he had been given by a friend who'd been there.

He got out in front of the private sex motel, run by some enterprising capitalist and came up to the door and was admitted after showing the card. With hand signals, his hands behind his back, and on top of his head like a prisoner, the manager got the message.

He was shown to a room. A young girl was brought in. Her hands were tied behind her back. She was striped almost naked and gagged. The Jg could feel himself getting hard as he listened to the girl trying to scream through the gag. As he watched her struggle vainly against the ropes, two men bounded her to the bed. It was their kind of fun. They were going to watch on close circuit T.V.

She was tied to the bed, her hands and arms lashed to the bed posts. Her knees bound to the side off the bed, her ankle and thigh flayed open, in such a way as to spread her legs up and out so after the Ltjg ripped off her panties and bra, there was no way she could resist him. He sat on the bed and listened to her moan and struggle as he slowly took off his shirt and pants. Her terrified young eyes watched the Jg's hand rise to strike her. The men heard the slaps and cries and knew it was time to go to the T.V. room.

It was the morning of the special surfing liberty, Me and Pancho reveillied at 0400. I got the old board from its hidden space among the shoring and we walked off the ship in liberty whites each carrying an extra T-shirt and our Navy regulation bun huggers. We walked to the end of the dock security area, past Chinese guards, and then proceeded toward the bus and train station complex in the corner of the harbor through the deserted streets.

I leaned the board on a bench in a prominent place and we waited for Jade to arrive. Old men approached to peer at the surfboard and the foreign sailors. They stood at a close distance, cocked their heads, shifted their hips, smoked and stared at us.

"You know, here, I don't think it matters if we got our uniforms on or not, we still stick out like sore thumbs."

"They can see us coming for a mile away."

"At least they're not spitting on us and calling us baby killers."

"That's cuz they don't know us."

Just before the train left Jade arrived with the three tickets and led us, two sailors and the one surfboard through the turn stiles and onto the old train. We found seats and I secured the board. The train became partially crowded and at exactly the departure time posted, pulled out of the station. As the train shoved off Jade gave us plastic bags of hot and sweet soy bean milk and rice balls with deep fried bread in the middle.

The train made frequent stops as it worked along a river, climbing higher and higher into the green jungle covered mountains. The early morning air had a chill to it when from the top of the summit we began to come back down the other side. Jungle, then rice paddies, with an occasional water buffalo working with a conical hat farmer appeared as we sped through the valley and crossed a snaking river many times. It looked just like Vietnam.

The sun came up as the train moved along the river valley toward the sea. We got a glimpse of the sea at a place called Fulung but Jade kept us on the train and we moved inland again and up and through long tunnels then finally the train snaked along the side of a mountain next to the sea. There were terraced rice fields and small fishing villages.

Finally we got off in the tiny village of Da Hsi. We gave our tickets to the uniformed train station worker, left the station and crossed the road. I could see waves breaking in a large circular bay.

"Honey Moon Bay, have wave." Jade explained pointing to where I was already looking. "I go see family, You go waves." She gathered her possessions and began to walk off. "You come back station 1200."

I saw a set wave break right off the far point and peel a hundred yards into the bay. I waved at the departing Jade and then led Pancho in the other direction toward the beach.

"There must be some kinda storm pumping these waves." I remarked to Pancho as we walked off toward the breakers.

We took off our whites folded and placed them in a paper bag and I waxed down the board with candles I had brought. I took the board and paddled out into the waves. The waves that broke over me were warm and powerful and after a while I had made it out side where the wave started to crest and break. A larger set came in and I paddled further out, turned around and stroked for the looming face of water. I stroked hard and the wave picked me up then I was free falling down the face and making a turn along the azure tropical wall. I climbed and dropped along the wall gaining speed and just beating the crashing lip of the wave. I rode from the corner of the bay almost too the center. When the waves slowed I cut back into the hook, caught trim again and raced the crashing wave toward the shore. Finishing the ride I waved to Pancho who was playing in the shore break and then paddled back outside for another wave.

Later on the long train ride back to Keelung through the green flooded rice paddies I watched Pancho and Jade sleep in the sweltering heat. Pancho was sunburnt. Jade was beautiful in slumber. I looked outside the train at a passing crowded ornate Chinese graveyard that sprawled alongside of a Loma by the sea. I couldn't get my mind off the Da Nang Harbor during the northeastern monsoons of 1967 and 1968, during the Tet Offensive. The New Year offensive that caused President Johnson not too run for reelection in 1968.

I remembered Johnson's speech. "I shall not seek, and I will not accept the nomination of my party for another term as your president." I had been surfing sloppy waves at China Beach in Da Nang in the spring. I had survived Tet at Hue. I had worked a 12 hours night shift offloading ammo in the Danang Bay. 12 hours a day, seven days a week, 30 days a month, one month on days and one month nights. When the night shift finished I hitched a ride to the beach and rode some waves on Velzy pop outs the Aussies had brought in.

I had lost my board and had swum into get it. I heard, over the beach speakers, Johnson's voice. I retrieved the board from the now shallow water and had taken it up near the water's edge and sat down listening to my Commander in Chief.

Johnson was getting out. He was leaving a half a million Americans troops in Vietnam but he himself was getting out. I had a very bad taste in his mouth.

I got some more waves then got back to the hootch for some sleep. I remembered the monsoon season. Then the hatch teams were launched from the beach in Da Nang harbor in little flat bottom LCVPs and ventured forth into the big swells of the North Eastern monsoons. We would fight the gray on coming eight foot swells to make it near the bay mouth, and turn around gunning the diesels and riding the swells back toward the Ammo ships that were moored or anchored in the bay.

The teams would scurry up the swinging Jacob's ladders that hung from the bow of the merchant ship. We would go up one at a time on the swell's upswing, in the pouring rain. Once on the wet decks we broke into the holds and off loaded the ammo into waiting barges, or other small craft alongside. The ship's cargo was too volatile to be off loaded at pier side. If the ship was attacked and blown up at the pier the whole facility would go with it. If the ship got blown up seaside, they'd only loose an expendable hatch team. Some U.S. merchant crews were very warm to the Navy, allowing them inside the super structure and even inviting us to eat. Other merchant crew prohibited the swabbies from entering the super structure and even had us defecate and urinate on little open wooden platforms that hung off the gunnels. I had seldom gone aboard a merchant ship by way of the gang plank, always come on board via Jacob ladders or cargo nets hung over the side.

We said good bye at the station and tired and sun burnt wobbly made for the wharf. Entering the secured area of the docks from the crowded streets we noticed the Topa was no longer there. We met a line handling party.

"What ship did you work?" asked Pancho.

In chorus they replied. "The Topa." We started to run and coming around the corner saw her, already under way and heading for the harbor mouth.

Stunned, we looked to the decks of our ship. Everyone was yelling and pointing to the end of the quay where a small Taiwanese harbor tug waited with her diesel engines belching white gray smoke.

We broke in a foot race for the end of the pier. Being stranded in Keelung might have at first seemed like a good idea, except when one thought of the lack of money in our pockets, pay records to get any more being on the ship. There was the problem of the potential disciplinary action that could result in missing ship's movement.

We sprinted down the dock toward the tug. I with the bagged surfboard under my arm was losing the race to Pancho. He flew off the pier and landed with a certain grace on the deck of the little tug, being caught by one of the Taiwanese before almost being carried by momentum into Keelung Harbor. I followed, and went aboard.

With the two bluejackets and one surfboard on board the line was released and the tug pulled into the channel to try and catch the Topa who was gaining way. The Topa rigged a cargo net over the gunnel as the tug pulled alongside. Pancho scrambled up the cargo net. I paused for a moment looking at the board. Someone threw me a line and I secured my board to it. Someone began hoisting the board away. I now climbed the net to the gunnel.

The little tug pulled away, opening a gap between her and the side of the Topa.

I swung over the gunnel to see the Lt.jg take the line that held the surfboard away from Reyes. He looked me in the eyes then let the board fall back toward the water. I leaned over the gunnel in time to see the board hit the water and get washed along the side of the ship and finally sucked into the screws, the propellers of the ship. There was a sharp crack. In the trailing white water of the ship's wake I thought I saw the pieces of the broken board bobbing in the whiteness.

I made it down the passageway and down the series of ladders to my bunk, in shock. I climbed the chains to my top lair and crapped out. Nothing was ever said about our being late and I never mentioned it either. Only two reasons were even proffered for the ship's early departure. There was a typhoon approaching or the Captain wanted to get to the combat zone before the month ended for the extra pay.

CHAPTER 5

Deployment: Yankee Station, Gulf of Tonkin.

Topa dutifully steamed south and west toward the Tonkin Gulf, and Vietnam. It wasn't the first time she'd been there. She in fact knew the waters well. The old lady had under weigh replenished the original destroyers who were allegedly attacked by North Vietnamese torpedo boats in 1964. Then she had supplied the Maddocks and had unrepped the Seventh Fleet that was gathering to do their worst against North Vietnam. It wasn't the first time for me either. But now was 1969. Johnson had high tailed it. Martin Luther King Jr. had been murdered while I was still in Da Nang. Bobby Kennedy had been killed just after I'd come back off my 30 day leave, little more than a month after I had returned to the world.

President Nixon was now Commander in Chief. He was looking for "Peace with Honor". Even stupid enlisted men like me were starting to figure out what was to come. He had proposed troop withdrawals. The antiwar sentiment was rising in the States and the war seemed all but lost after the Tet. It continued so "Peace with Honor" could be found. 1969 was the bloodiest year of the Viet Nam war.

It became hot on deck and hotter in the compartments and cargo holds as the old ship headed south and west toward Nam. The sea shimmered and glistened with heat as flying fish leaped in front of the ship and flew for twenty or thirty meters or more then dove back into the sea as others jumped and soared for seconds then splashed beneath the surface. Out to sea porpoises approached and circled the ship leaving only the dead body of a shark in their wake.

A couple of days later, before the first under way replenishment, the hatch teams were mustered for a practice at the hatch squares.

I looked over my team in the searing musty heat of the deep unlit hold.

There was Reyes, Big Keoke, Heavy, and Little Aqui and Black Doaks. Doaks and Aqui stood as far as they could from each other.

Training in the Navy was different. I had attended DOD schools with my tribe, the Navy brats. Quaint stilted Quonset hut classrooms. I had been to boot camp, SK'A" School, Survival, Escape, Resistance, and Evasion training, In A school I learned the intricacies of the naval supply system so I could go to Nam where I counted two thousand pound bombs individually. I had been to survival school in the desert, to go to the tropics. The first time I boarded a merchant ship full of ammo seaside in the Da Nang harbor monsoon rains poured down and a large swell was pouring into the big mouth bay. From the pitching and rolling decks of the LCVP, the only training for going up the free swing Jacob's ladder had been:

"Watch this guy." Now it's your turn." I sped up the rope ladder, hand over hand, trying to ascend quickly so that the next swell didn't raise the landing craft high knock me off the line and pitch me into the sea. I had seen one sailor who went up too slow, was popped by the gunnel of the bobbing landing craft on the upswing and tossed into the sea. That was the last we saw of him. Offload operations were not halted. The mission was more important.

I thought my own hatch team should know what they had to do before they actually had to do it. They stood in front of me in the hatch's square, sullen, suppressed, hating the Navy and sometimes each other, part of a defeated, demoralized military struggling for a lost cause that was already being parlayed away in Paris.

Duty was duty and there was no way to get out of it. Best do it quickly and get back to the main deck. Everyone on the team had personal strengths as well as weaknesses. We were all young and in shape except for Heavy who was paunchy and winded easily, but had an eye for paper work.

"OK Heavy, you take the clip board, with the list of the stuff we gotta break out and the number we need of each item. See the list? You call out the item and numbers to us." I said handing the clipboard and the list to Heavy. He took it willingly, even joyfully. He was going to skate again.

"First thing we gotta do is open the hold." As he said this Reyes and Keoke, started taking the long hatch boards off the hold and walking them from the middle of the hold to the edge. There they stacked them, carefully securing them in place. I wasn't worried about Reyes or Keoke. Reyes was quick and had done it before on other cruises and Keoke could pick up an anchor link with each hand and carry it while it took two others to pick up half the load, and he'd done it before to. Aqui had done it to.

"Keoke, you musta screwed up to be sent down from deck to be put in the hold?"

"Da chief was yelling at me, and I told him, `But chief, the missionaries, dey neva tol us bout dat. He didn't think it was too funny. He ship my okole down to hell here with you haoles."

Heavy and Aqui followed their lead and I and Doaks alternated, soon freeing the hatch, opening it up so that the men could climb down another tier. Reyes and I made sure that the long flat boards were secured well.

"We don't want these mothers falling on us." He said.

Once the hatch boards were secured with the lines that Bear and I had spliced coming across the Pacific, the team went down into the depths of the hold.

"All don safety hats." I ordered. "The quicker we get this done, the quicker we can get back to the main deck."

"Ah, we gotta wear them hats?"

"Yeah, these mothers lose their steering, or one of the other ships lose their steering, we don't wanna be way down here." If we are, we don't want nothing falling on us, but if it does, I guess this hats will help some, hey Reyes?"

"Might happen. Might save your worthless lifer ass."

The thought sobered us up and we looked around and looked up toward the main deck that was still covered in darkness.

"OK. Heavy, will call um out and count um, then we sending them up. Me and Aqui will search for the stuff and I'll dig it out and toss to Aqui, but if anybody else sees the stuff, call it out," I instructed.

"Like I said the quicker..."

"Yeah, yeah, we got the picture..." I really didn't outrank anybody on the team. Reyes and Heavy were third class crow bearers. But it was my team and my responsibility. They took my lead, although uneasily. As the team saw that I was going to bust my ass too, that I was going to work with them, not just sit on my ass and call out orders, they went along better.

Reyes interrupted.

"I'll set up the pallets and the cargo nets with Keoke." Keoke grunted an affirmative.

"Doaks, you're the middle man." Keoke said. "You're between me and Aqui. Doaks held his hands out pleadingly.

"You bloods don't understand, I'm too heavy for light work and too light for heavy work, I don't belong in your Navy, Man'. There were boos and catcalls as Doaks' jived into position. "Especially you Semmes, you're the biggest lifer I ever seen."

I thought Doaks did fit nicely between little Aqui and giant Keoke. I, on one end, knew where the stuff was and Reyes on the other was quick and strong and could visualize just how the stuff could be stacked for maximum efficiency, how the bags and boxes could be placed. And he could do it quickly, with no foolishness.

They could all feel the heat of the tropics. It was going to get hot down there, hotter than hell.

"Strip to the waist from now on. We'll do it on the level where we first break in and stack out hatch boards. Hard hats and steel toes are must for every one and that includes you, Heavy".

"Yeah, yeah, I know the routine, chief." and he did. "I don't plan on dying for the Navy." He tapped the navy issue black pen against the clipboard. It was going to be the heaviest thing he was going to have to pick up.

"Semmes, I'm a short timer. Less than a hundred days, then it's your Navy." They all laughed and figured days mentally. I was afraid to count.

A day later in the darkness of the early predawn morning the hatch teams had been fed and called away. The deck force was working their tails off and preparing to the send the stuff across the scant distance to the can or the carrier that was coming along side at 12 knots. They needed servicing. I had picked up the list from Pancho, who had gotten it from the chief, in the cargo office on the main deck. The list had been radioed over from the client ship. Bear and the other hatch team leaders had been there. Once I had the list I mustered my team and led them down into the hold to break it open.

It took the team a few minutes to get organized.

"What is the first item?" I yelled up to Heavy.

"Flour, white, sixty pound sacks." The quantity followed.

"They must do a load of baking on that ship."

"Here it is." I yelled and tore down some of the shoring then muscled a sack in the air and threw it at Aqui.

The sack weighted more than half as much as Aqui and acted like a cross body block on the little Filipino who went down immediately. I laughed but Aqui was to his feet in an instant, pissed at me. He was being helped up by Doaks.

"Fook," he said with his little accent, "Semmes, you TOSS it, don't throw it." I half crawled over, crouched in the dark hold, as was everybody else and tried to apologize.

"Easy does it." Doaks said to me. Patting my shoulder.

I started again and this time I tossed it. Aqui was ready.

I didn't wait to see the sack go down the line to the hatch's square where Keoke was handling it off to Reyes who bent at the waist stacking it. I dug for another tossing it to Aqui who moved it to Doaks and then to Keoke and Reyes. Reyes called out the number he'd stacked on the wooden pallet and Heavy marked the clipboard. Soon I didn't have to look and neither did Reyes, the cargo just appeared or was caught, and in this way the cargo snaked from the deep hold to the hatch's square.

The sun broke through the darkened hatched square as it was open by the deck force. The cargo hook whined and whirled toward us at the bottom of the hold and jerked to a stop just above the stacked pallet. The announcements from the Topa's P.A. system echoed down in the depths of the hold but were unintelligible to the sailors. We knew however that the ships were coming alongside Topa.

Reyes and Keoke joined by Doaks, who was close, being in the middle of the line, and Heavy, one hand on the clip board, the other free, hustled to the hatch square to help hook up the cargo net rungs around the ship's cargo hook. That done Reyes signaled it aloft. He steadied the load for and instant, then quickly started laying the pallets and nets for the next load in the hatch square.

Soon our naked bodies glistened with sweat, black, brown, tan and white. We were soon covered with a layer of white flour that seeped from the bags as they were hefted to the pallets. The flaky power clung to our skins and turned to dough as the flour and salty sweat mixed.

The more we loaded the cargo the better we became, the faster we worked. Different colors didn't matter, races, or cultures didn't matter. With the flower caked on our bodies we were all white anyway.

We worked on and on, grunting and humping, crouched in the hold or ducking in the hatch's square in the intense tropical heat of the Asian summer of '69. The air was full of dust. Our bodies dripped with sweat and were caked with grime.

The cargo went up on the hook to be staged on the deck, out of the way and then sent to other ships.

The Navy under way replenishment at sea, refueling, receiving ammo and food allowed the most powerful Naval force in the world to remain at sea and not have to go back to port for supplies or services. Mail, even personnel could be transferred at sea. The two, three or more ships moving at near top speed, in tandem, passed lines, shooting them to one another, then hooked them up to winches and booms and boatswain mates transferred the cargo. The cargo went from the holds to the deck in nets then across the ocean on lines hooked between the ships. The teams on the other ship pulled in the cargo and transferred it below decks.

It disappeared, piece by piece into the storage areas like a line of ants, from one sailor to another.

From within the holds of the Topa the hatch teams could hear the garbled P.A. systems of the approaching ship and the Topa giving instructions and sounding sirens of alarm, and the BOOM as the shot lines were propelled across the water to the other ship. Sometimes they knew there would be a ship on both sides of the Topa in a Naval ménage a trois, a high sea trinity.

The team worked unceasingly until Heavy yelled out.

"That's it."

We climbed up the ladders out of the hold and quickly unhooked the hatch boards from the side where they had been stored and stacked and laid them back, covering the tiers of the hold as we ascended to the main deck.

"Secure." I said as they reached the level before the main deck and put on the last hatch boards.

"And good job, boys." I said to all of them.

"Semmes, you see a boy, you come and kick his ass." Doaks said his body caked with white flour, his tired muscles tensed.

"Hey, you took it wrong man. GOOD JOB is what I said. I ain't messing with you. Now get outta here and go rest. I bet we the first one done." I said with a little pride. Doaks relaxed.

I didn't have to tell the men to hide. They had done a job, but if anyone saw them, especially an officer or a chief, they'd give them something to do. 'Since they weren't doing anything.' This would be especially true for the crow less men, strikers, like Doaks and Keoke and Aqui. Doaks moved slowly up the narrow steel ladder to the main deck. He was beat. I followed him up, then wove my way down the crowded deck to Bear's hold and then lowered myself down the ladder to the level where Bear was working, to bare a hand.

Bear was there, holding his clip board and directing Peaches, and the Big cook Bubba, among others in the team, during the off load. I jumped in and gave Peaches and others a hand loading the gear and hooking up the cargo net to the hook.

It was work I didn't have to do but getting done and everybody out of the hold was important to me. Too many guys would have been in the way, but an extra hand, that was helpful. Then everybody could rest. Besides, Bear was a friend and getting the cargo out was duty. The quicker it was got out, the happier the Commander might be. It takes all hands to tie up the ship, or to do the ships work, my father had always said and that was what I was doing. Helping the ship do its work. I grabbed a box, placed it on the pallet and then helped hook up.

Aqui found his way to Officers Country and started to help his bros prepare food in the wardroom. Because the work, the first days of the unrep, the chief steward had mandated that the officers be given cold cuts. The officer wouldn't eat Filipino food, like rice and chicken wings and other delicacies. The officers messed with the stewards and the stewards messed with them, but not directly. They ate the Captain's ice cream with their hands, for example and laughed with revengeful guffaws in the cold quiet of the freeze box doing it. If you mess with someone who cooks your food, you're asking for it.

When the stewards were pissed the officers got cold cuts, cold cuts and cold cuts again. If the officers had the duty he could wander into the crew's mess and eat with the crew and hope that Robbie was cooking that day. If he didn't at least the mostly raw baked spuds would be hot. When an officer came to the crew's mess he was kept away from, like someone with something worse than the Black Death. Some bolder sailors would ask....

"Hey sir, what you doing down here?"

And the reply would be....

"Cold cuts again. I came down for some hot food." Some of the crew mumbled that was against regulations. Regulations were only for the crew and not the officers.

Doaks was trying to make it to his bunk for a few winks when the chief saw him.

"Boy, come here," said the chief. Doaks said nothing about the BOY. He couldn't wise off to the chief like he could to Semmes, who was just a third class.

"You go stand your fire room watch." Doaks had forgotten he had the watch, and rolled out of his soiled bunk and bent over to tie his work boots up again. The Chief wasn't quite done.

"Then when you are done with that come back here, pack you gear and report to Supply. They done assigned you to mess cooking again. I hope you like it in the scullery." Doaks didn't say anything, but to himself was screaming.

"What the scullery again?" Doaks had picked up on the fact that in the Navy people thought of him as dull and stupid and he did nothing overtly to change their minds. He did everything to oblige them. Doaks stood his watch, then came back and moved his locker to Supply and got a bunk there among the mess cooks. By that time as he had just crapped out on his new bunk the mess cooks were called away. Doaks was tired, but he went with them.

Keoke had walked out on deck to get a fresh air whiff and as soon as he did he heard....

"Pineapple." It was the Big Red, the Boatswain second class calling him. He had, like the rest of the deck force, life jackets and hard hats over his dungarees.

"Get your ass out here and help us, no wait, you got the fantail watch, get your big dumb tail back there and relieve the watch."

"But Boats," Keoke said in all seriousness, "Da missionaries, dey neva tole us bout dat." It was becoming his mantra. Red looked at him for a second in disbelief then turned back to his work. Keoke turned and left, ambling down the crowded deck aft to relieve the watch, he smiled to himself. He wondered why nobody thought that was funny.

Reyes found his top bunk in engineering and climbed up dirty, lay down and closed his eyes and dozed, listening to the sound of the winches whining above his head and thought of Alison's young firm body so far away. He had nothing to do until water hours. Maybe once they got to the P.I. there would be mail. Or he could even call home. He could manage it. He had to talk to her, had to hear her voice again. There'd only been one letter for him in Taiwan.

Bear and I, done, and the holds secured, came on deck. The underway replenishment continued. Another destroyer, a tin can, came bobbing up through the waves of the Tonkin Gulf and shot lines were sent over to hook and rig the two ship together.

"Hey, you two. Report." The call came from the junior officer of the first division deck, a bitter washed out air dale. "You're a part of this ship so bear a hand." The officer told two of his seamen to take a break and for Semmes and the Bear to don their jackets and helmets and help with the unrep. We both thought of protesting but decided against it. It was late in the afternoon and the sea's face was wrinkled by a late sea breeze. The men on the winches had been working since the early morning, taking the cargo and putting it on deck and then transferring it across to the decks of the client ships. They were tired.

Bear and I hooked up the pallet on deck and then helped the deck apes steady the cargo with lines. I approached the swinging pallet to release it for its journey over to the can when, just as I reached the pallet, the tired winch man jerked the load. Suddenly where I was grabbing there was nothing. I fell head first into the sea.

I found myself taking a long free fall toward the waves. Then there was impact. It was like wiping out on a big wave. A rush of full adrenaline filled my body and as I surfaced I did a Duke Kahanamoku Australian crawl outboard to escape being sucked into the ship's screws. I didn't want to follow my surfboard's fate. I didn't stop stroking outboard until the ship churned past a few yards from me at 12 knots. I was just out of reach of the pulsating pounding screws of the ship as she chugged by, her big hungry propeller chopped the sea her wake washing over me like a wave.

Out of immediate danger I put my thumb high in the air signaling to the ship and my shipmates that I had made it past the screws.

Keoke standing the Fan Tail watch threw a marker and life buoy and sounded the alarm, which was already being passed through the ship: MAN OVER BOARD, EMERGENCY BREAK

AWAY. The ships had to break apart, and turn around and go back and get the shipmate without losing him or running over him in the wind wrinkled Tonkin Gulf. The ship's horn signaled emergency break away with six long hard pulls. The deck forced worked frantically to free the two cuddled ships. Keoke tried to keep the shipmate in sight, hard, because he was already disappearing from sight in ruffles of the sea. The guy had looked like Semmes, Keoke thought.

Reyes heard the emergency breakaway signal, dressed and scrambling toward the main deck. He didn't know why emergency break away had been sounded, but didn't want to take any chances. Perhaps one of the ships had their steering fail and was at that second careening toward the Topa, or her toward the other ship and would collide right where Reyes slept near the bulkhead on the starboard side.

He came on deck and met Bear who pointed out Semmes, just barely a speck, a small gray dot in a great gray sea, quickly disappearing aft.

The two ships struggled forward, trying to disengage.

"Man overboard." was all Bear said pointing. "It's Semmes."

Heavy startled awake in the hidden recesses of his storeroom, and made it to the main deck and observed the boatswain mates still trying to disengage the two ships. Both Heavy and Reyes went up the starboard side. It was all training.

Aqui broke from the wardroom and walked on the decks of Officers Country, and looked out to sea.

Doaks in the hot noise of the engine room, knew there was a problem, but could not leave his post. He stood there in the one hundred and forty-degree heat and looked around at the ancient plant that powered his ship. She pulsed and vibrated and the gauges jumped. She was older than he was by seven or eight years. She was twenty- six years old. Was it like riding in a car that old? Yeah, except for if this baby broke down and she was doing twelve knots and hooked up to another ship, all hell was going to break loose. Sweat ran down his forehead and he grabbed the rails hold for some support.

Finally the ships broke apart and both circled around to look for the man over board. To those peering with the naked eye he had long since disappeared into the dark gray pleats of the Gulf of Tonkin. The ships had gone a considerable distance.

I swam over and hung onto the long poled marker devise with the red flag at the top and watched the ships get smaller as they steamed away from me. The water was warm. My dirty dungarees became heavy. I had lost my hat in the fall. I thought of sharks in the warm waters of the Tonkin Gulf. I thought of being picked up by a North Vietnamese fishing boat and spending forever in a communist prison camp. Finally I could see that the two ships were breaking apart, and beginning to circle back toward me. I thought about getting run over by either one or the other of the ships. But thank God they were coming back.

The Topa, circled in a tighter arc than the destroyer trying to keep the man insight, fixing his last position in the gathering darkness. They proceed with a quick caution. They wanted to get the sailor but not run him over. Who knew if sharks were following the ships? Trash is thrown off the fantail only at certain times to prevent a long trail of garbage for the enemy or sharks to follow.

Men over board were sometimes never recovered. Topa launched her boat and picked me up almost at dusk. I was wet, tired and in shock but damn glad when I was back on the decks of the Topa. The word was passed through the scuttlebutt grape vine from the bridge that the sailor had been recovered from the Tonkin Gulf. It was too late to continue operations and they were postponed for resumption at dawn on the morrow.

The crew was in a nasty mood, because the officers were in a nasty mood. The scuttlebutt from the standing watch during the unrep was that it was the Topa's winch men fault that the cargo was jerked and that caused me to fall over board. Plus I was inept for falling overboard.

Topa's captain was incensed at the slow response to emergency break away. A few more minutes and darkness might have doomed the sailor and imagine the paper work. The terrible ship's movie was canceled and it was announced that the crew had been using too much water and that water hours were to be reduced again.

Everyone looked around at each other.

"Who took a shower?" Bird started screaming.

"What bastard took a shower, who's been drinking water again?" If anyone had used any water, nobody was saying. Everybody was given the same blank stares back that they got.

"No drinking water, you ass holes." Bird said and then screamed out a high cackling, crazy laugh.

After being released by Doc in sick bay, I joined Heavy and Reyes to go to the bow to blow a joint in the cool, fresh air of the night at sea. There were a million stars above and we sat on the deck below the gun tubs and cupped our hands around the joint, took drags and then blew the smoke into the air. Heavy had had enough of getting loaded in below decks, in those confined spaces, and needed to get up to the freedom of the main deck. The emergency breakaway that awoke him from stupor had frightened him. He'd thought the sea was going to be pouring in on him at any time.

We watched the whiteness of the swells breaking off the bow but didn't talk much. We got into the rise and fall of the ship and the whiteness of the waves crashing off the bow. We drank in the clean fresh air of the sea's night breezes and watched the stars pitch and roll in the black sky. The night air was refreshing, and life giving, so different from the cramped, stale stinking compartments where we lived or the deep holds where we worked.

Walking back aft to the ship fitters shack to see a magazine that Reyes had, we were stopped by an unofficial messenger from the bridge. It was one of the deck apes.

"Hey, tell whoever's blowing `J's on the bow to belay, because the guys on watch can whiff the smoke on the bridge."

"Sure, we'll tell if we see um." Reyes said.

"Thanks for passing the word." Depending on the wind's direction, we weren't going to be able to blow any joints on the bow anymore. If we wanted to get high and watch the stars or see the waves break off the bow we would have to get loaded first, and then go to the bow. We walked on the outside rail of the ship, along the super structure and passed number four and then passed number five holds. There were small groups of sailors on the deck hidden among the winches.

"Psst." Someone called to them. It was the Bear, getting high with Keoke and some others. He pointed forward toward the superstructure, indicating we should look higher on the 0-1 level. The Ltjg was standing there smoking a cigarette.

The Asian summer days passed in a timeless, grueling orgy of work with seemingly unceasing early reveilles and late taps. The crew moved to the clang of the ship's bells and the shrill piercing whistle of the bosun's pipe, ordering us about. We worked in a void, never knowing where we were exactly, which direction we were going or how long it was to go on. We mustered on the deck or in the darkness of the hold to break out the cargo, unrep during the day, and then worked at night to prepare for the next day. If there were breaks in the routine, they were spent at General Quarter stations or fighting imaginary fires. The days flowed into weeks of watch standing, ships work and under weigh replenishments. The crew only knew that it was hot, and that water hours were continually being reduced, that the food was bad and that they were to blame, cajoled and objurgated for their lack of performance. If it wasn't Decks fault it was Engineering's or Supply's. We worked as hard as we could, continually drank coffee off the mess decks when we could. We were too tired to think of much else.

The snipes in the engine room ate reds to sleep and whites to go on watch and some even shot the stuff, tying off and putting the needles in their arms. The deck boys ate the little white pills and drank smuggled on booze to sleep. Operations and communications smoked a little dope and drank a little and stood their watches. Supply smoked its' hash and its' dope until it ran out.

In the baking heat of the Asian continental summer, shorts were allowed. The word came down from the executive officer to the yeoman, then to the crew in the scuttlebutt chain of command. Khaki shorts were allowed for those who wore the low cut black cordovans. Men wearing work boots would have to remain in long blue dungarees.

This amounted to Communications, Operations and the officers donning cool khakis shorts. The rest of the crew, Supply, Deck and Engineering were denied this privilege. This made Operation and Communications look like the officers and further divided them from the crew. Supply, Deck and Engineering began to loathe this small group of men, who had somehow joined the officers.

Reyes jumped from his rack one morning before reveille and quickly dressed in his dungarees pants and work boots. He had only a white skivvy shirt on. He and his plastic cup went to the mess decks that were next to the engineering compartment, for a cup of coffee, before the chow line formed. As he walked onto the mess decks, the Chief Master at Arms, the big African American first class the other brothers call an Uncle Tom, but not to his face, bade Reyes stop and return for a dungaree shirt.

Reyes swore, a Chicano word directed at the big African American.

"Miyate." The big Chief Master at Arms approached Reyes belligerently.

"What did you say to me?" He queried. Reyes was both out gunned and out ranked but still thought about going for it. The only thing that kept him off his toes was thoughts of getting back with Alison. He didn't need any brig time, so he backed off.

"I can work on deck, or in the holds without a dungaree shirt, but I gotta have one for a cup of joe?" He said putting his face into the CMAA's who now stood in front of him, badge and all.

"That's right," CMAA said. Reyes turned away and went back to get his dungaree shirt. By the time he returned there was already a long line forming for chow. His addiction to coffee would have to wait.

The crew's laundry had been suspended along with a complete reduction of water hours. The men could drink water but it had to be sucked out of the water spigot. Nobody changed clothes. They kept the same dungaree pants for work in the holds and a shirt for muster on the decks. Some tried to wash their dirty pants by tying a line to them and dragging the pants behind the ship where the bouncing and pounding made them clean but salty. Some articles of clothing were dedicated to the deep this way. The stink and sweat, smells of piss and defecation permeated the crew's quarters, and was made even riper by the heat. Dirty work clothes were hung on the bunk chains and used when the hatch teams were called away. Semmes and Bear fell back on habits they had learned in Vietnam. They wore no skivvy shorts. They wore no skivvy shirts when they could get away with it. Sores and boils developed on their skin, in their crotches.

The officers continued to walk around in freshly laundered and pressed khakis. The spots and stains on the Jg's khaki shirts still tipped off Supply to what the officers were eating.

One day at quarters, the Jg had an announcement.

"Men, we are going to be picking up four Filipino workers off the ship we'll be unrepping tomorrow and we will transport them to Subic Bay. These people are dirty and untrustworthy, if you have any valuables you wish to safe guard, please bring them to me and I will hold them for you, safe, until we reach port. Dismissed." The men were dismissed and started to chatter.

"Hey Scarfi, you gonna take your valuables up to the Jg's stateroom for safe keeping?"

"I got something for that Jg, something to put in his mouth and suck on."

"I bet those Filipino workers are more trust worthy and honest than that Jg is."

"How can that dude say that with all the Filipinos in the division?"

"We cook his food, shine his shoes, clean his stateroom and do everything but wipe his ass and he says we are untrustworthy."

"He don't know no better, he's just a dumb racists." They wander off to commence ship's work. The next day the workers came aboard, being transferred at sea, the same way the cargo was sent over, but this time they came back in little bosun chair seats that the deck apes had rigged. They came over one by one strapped to the chair from one of the high tech new tin cans. They were technicians, all G.S. 12 and up. One was a white American, the rest were really nice fellows who took time and showed Supply their skill by working on the ventilation, making it work a lot better. The white guy said he could have kicked one of the officers out of his stateroom, but didn't mind staying with the crew. They found little bunks wherever they were available, and never complained. No one, it turned out, took any valuables up for safeguarding with the Jg.

Finally the fleets hunger had been satiated and the aging ship and her tired crew broke away from the Gulf of Tonkin and coast of Vietnam and the ships of the line, bound for the Philippines. It was a couple days chug across the South China Sea. The day the Topa pulled into Subic was intensely hot and windless. The air was humid and heavy and the bay reflected the piercing white sunlight off its surface. The sky was perfectly clear and blue except for some virginal white powdery clouds that hung above verdant green hills. It was plain hot and humid in the windless bay and the Topa pulled in at General Quarters. The sleeves and collars were all buttoned down and the trousers all tucked into socks as the sailors stood GQ under hard metal pots which saved them from the sun, though they sweated profusely. They pulled into the berth next to other American ships, crews looked incredulously at the Topa's crew, snickered but didn't run it in to the ground. Ships coming off the line tended to be in a bad mood and prone to violence. The crew could have endured anything for it knew that in a few hours, after the sea and anchor detail had been secured, and all the life support systems were hooked up, there was going to be liberty in the wild Olongapo City, Subic Bay, and the Philippines.

CHAPTER 6

Subic Bay, Philippines

"Give me Liberty or give me death."
                                          -Patrick Henry

"Sailor vises are a clear expression of the laws of nature. They seem to come less from evil desires than from happiness of spirit at being free after a long time on the ship at sea."
                                          -Herman Melville

One of the best things about the wide open liberty town of Olongapo, was that the Topa officers were restricted to the base in Subic. The reason for this was that for a few pesos or for nothing the little Negritos of the mountains would use their blowguns to assassinate them. To the men it was an appealing thought, a nice poison dart stuck in the Jg's neck.

Bear, Heavy, Keoke, Doaks, and Reyes, all left the ship together and had angled first for the snack bar on the base where they scored hamburgers and French fries that were every bit as good as home.

Aqui and I would have gone with them, but the Jg had summarily restricted us to the ship.

"The Jg could interrupt a good bowl movement." Heavy said as they ate.

"He is a good bowl movement."

"Where we going after chow?" Keoke asked.

"I'll be going to the Soul Club." Doaks said and it wasn't an invitation. It had been a miracle that Doaks had gotten off the ship. He was going to make the most of it.

"I'll be leaving you honky mothers all alone, so I can get together with the brothers." He was going to an all black club. Things were very specialized in Olongapo City.

Reyes was the first to leave the group, and he did it before they left the base.

"I'm going over to the Base Exchange, see if I can get anything for the casa." Reyes said, looking down at his folded hands, pensively. Reyes did not feel excited to be in Olongapo City. He was rather concerned about the lack of correspondence that he received from Alison. There had been just one letter from her and they had been gone from the States for over six weeks. There should have been more waiting for him in Keelung. There was the probability that the Navy mail was messed up and had not caught them as yet. This was the first time he had left her on a West Pac cruise. The other times he had gone over seas she had still been in high school. She had written. He assumed that the mail was lost or that she was involved in studying for her finals and sooner or later he would hear from her. There was a pain in his chest thinking about this that had nothing to do with the greasy food they were eating. He would go over to the telephone exchange or maybe the Mars phone and see if he could get through.

He wished he could be like Semmes in a way. Semmes never worried about mail call. In fact he had gotten letters so seldom that the storekeeper never even went to mail call. He seemed to feel like that if there were letters for him they would find their way to his bunk. There was no excitement for him when the magic words "MAIL CALL" bounced off the bulkheads of the compartment when they were in port. He wasn't about to go out of his way, to stop what he was doing and wait, crowded around some bunk. The chances of Semmes getting a letter were almost nonexistent. Very occasionally there would be a letter from his parents, with a Surfer magazine, other than that he received nothing. Even the college Semmes had written to, requesting information and a catalog had never replied. Semmes had figured it had been the APO address that had done it.

"They don't want no swabbies, or ex swabbies going to that school." Semmes said. That was the last they heard about it. Semmes, since he never got mail he learned to care less about it.

Reyes on the other hand was crazy for the mail, like so many of the other men. It was their connection with home, their link to the outside. Reyes made it to the Base Exchange and aimlessly looked at the stuff and thought of Alison. He thought about calling home, calling her, hearing her voice, but put it off for a few days, he'd be patient. He didn't want to jump the gun.

Heavy, Bear and Keoke got up and left the snack bar and went out the gate of the base. The first street outside was paved, but as they got further off from the base the streets turned to dirt and gravel, and mud.

"I'm still hungry." Heavy said, "Let's go get us a taco."

"Hey, man", Bear said, "This ain't California you know."

"You don't know much about the Philippines." Heavy led them down a street that was still covered with mud puddles from the rain the day before and then into a sizable restaurant, where Heavy ordered tacos for everybody in passable Tagalog, with a young and demure waitress.

The boss, a Chinese Filipino, when he saw who it was, stopped what he was doing and came around the counter and greeted Heavy personally, after telling one of the helpers something that made him quickly disappear. Heavy replied fluently. Bear was impressed.

"Heavy, I didn't know you could speak it, sounds pretty good."

"Yeah, there's a lot of dialects here in the P.I. but Tagalog is a widely used one." Heavy said.

Just then one of the most beautiful women Bear had ever seen came into the room, walked over to Heavy and threw her arms around him and kissed him on the side of his fat round head, then on the lips, passionately.

Heavy for his part, took a wad of money out of his pocket and stuffed the bills in her small delicate hands. Nobody had ever seen Heavy give anybody any money unless he noted it down in his account book.

Heavy put his hands around her waist and the tiny, well-shaped women sat on Heavy's lap for an instant, then got a chair from the next table which was abandoned, and joined the sailors.

Keoke laughed and Bear dropped his jaw.

"This here is my fiancée, Anna, this is a crazy, big galoot is a lumber jack from the north woods, Bear, and you know Keoke. She smiled at the sailors. They stared back.

"Howdy ma'am, Glad to meet you." Bear said. Heavy explained that Anna's family was Chinese Filipinos and that she was a Hong Kong citizen with a British passport. They had business all over the South China Sea from Hong Kong to the P.I. Heavy had never mentioned Anna to any of the shipmates, except for Keoke, who had been on previous cruises. Heavy was a secretive guy. He had to be if he was going to be bringing and selling dope on the ship, running the slush fund and having pretty young women stored around. He couldn't be going off at the mouth all the time like some of the guys. He had to be discreet. Besides Anna just wasn't some trollop, she spoke beautiful English, two dialects of Chinese and was educated along with being a knockout.

Anna joined them for a while and Bear looked her over surreptitiously. She had an exquisite little frame and long black, thick hair with big round black eyes and some of the whitest healthiest teeth he'd ever seen. She was light and slim.

"We plan on getting married." Heavy said about the money.

"You know that in order to get married I gotta get permission through the chain of command, all the way through to the captain."

"I'm wondering how the Jg can mess it up for me."

"Yeah, the officers are racist, He kept Aqui on the ship today and who knows for what reason. Talk about biting the hand that feeds you. Dumb haole." Keoke said.

"Yeah, well stupid or not, he's got those little silver bars on his dirty khaki shirt."

Keoke interjected. "But you better watch that Jg though, even if you give him the chit he is liable to lose it. He'd lose his own ass hole if it wasn't connected to him." They all nodded in agreement and then embarked on lengthy tales detailing just how the Jg had lost their chits, a leave request, a special liberty, a standby. What the hell was he going to do with a request to marry, and to marry a Filipina, a foreigner, a gook, could only be imagined. Disapprove it at the very least. Then the discussion was over and Heavy cut it off.

"O.K. boys, I'm gonna run you out of here, me and the misses, well you know."

Bear and Keoke left the restaurant and looked for a bar. In Olongapo, they didn't have to look too far.

Aqui took his unofficial restriction to the ship as typical petty vindictiveness from the Jg. He'd seen the Jg do the same thing to Semmes and Heavy and others, when they were near home. The Jg himself had left the ship and was probably at the O club now having some Filipina. Or maybe he was too good to take a local girl, even for temporary sexual release. Who knew why officers did anything, especially the Jg?

Aqui did not worry about one liberty. The Jg had just taken his liberty card at the quarterdeck. He was told he had to stay on board and stand by to receive chow for the officer's mess. He had waited all afternoon and into the evening and still nothing had been delivered. He would wait cheerfully all through the night and the next day with a smiling face. Grinning. That's what they expected. There was no reason to get angry. At least it was stupid to show the officer that he was angry. The retribution would come later. The money would still be sent home to the family for support and education. He might never make third class, especially with this Jg aboard, but he would bide his time and soon the Jg would be transferred or he would. There were ways.

Bear and Keoke wandered around the streets of Olongapo. They found a bar and wandered in. The place was not well lit but there was a good band playing sweet and familiar music, the rock and roll and love songs of the late sixties. They barely reached a booth when a swarming, thronging noisy bevy of very young and very beautiful Filipinas overwhelmed them, laughing and trying to touch them, trying to get as close to the two sailors as they could, to make contact, to be chosen. It was overwhelming because stateside, especially in uniform, or with the short haircuts they were forced to wear, they were shunned.

There were so many pretty faces and tight slim bodies to choose from. Even for a normal civilian stateside, the selection would have been spectacular. For the sailors, after a long time at sea and generally rejected because of service to their country during an unpopular war, the dazzling selection of young women was intoxicating.

They ordered ice cold San Miguel beers that were so cold the bottles, when first brought to them, were frosted white and then slowly melted in the intense humidity. They sat in the heat in their liberty whites and nursed the brews, then Bear finished his in a few swigs, then they ordered another. They sat there, surrounded by the girls and trying to look them over and then catch the eye of the one they wanted. Soon they were paired off with likely ones and the others left forlorn until a few more sailors popped in the door.

They danced on the little dance floor of the club to a local band that played the favorites from home, better it seemed, or at least as good as the original artists.

During familiar songs they held the girls tight, remembering other girls, girls at home. The music was mostly slow but interspersed with fast ones. After a fast one, their uniforms were soaked.

Once a sailor picked a girl, the others left them alone. There was no butter flying, going from one girl to another at the same place. They felt light with the heavy steel toed boon dockers off their feet. Keoke held the little Filipina tight during the slow dances and could feel it rise through the thinness of the uniformed whites.

Back on the ship I lay in my rack and thought about the skivvy houses he had visited in Vietnam. One night he and some mates had gone to an out of bounds place. The more aggressive guys picked the young pretty girls first. I had taken last choice. They all went to quarters jammed packed by western standards. One took ones shoes before climbing in to the little cubicles. The only privacy was thin, almost sheer curtains pulled together at the entrance of the bunks. There was scarcely enough room to stretch out and I could have reached out and touched my shipmate across the "hall" he was so close. The beds were little bigger than the ship's racks. I slipped off my marine green fatigues and she got out of her white blouse and black silk pajama pants. I made love holding her arms high and away controlling her hands. I didn't want to wake up dead with my throat slit in some rice paddy.

Later some M.P.'s came to the hootch door. She covered my mouth with her hands and we listened to the arguments. There was Vietnamese QC and U.S. M.P.'s, marines since at that time in I Corp there was no regular army. With a greasing of the palm they were discouraged from looking any further. The Vietnamese QC were tough characters and the worst beating I ever saw administered was when I saw the QC beat up a woman on the streets of Tien Sha. It had been positively vicious and gruesome, with sticks to the ankles and other joins, and the woman screaming helplessly. Before dawn, we got up and shuffled off to work at the ammo ramps at the beach at Tien Sha. None of the sailors was found dead as was sometimes the case, found in the patties with a throat slit from ear to ear.

The guys who had picked first all come down with the clap, and within weeks I saw them screaming at the urinals while trying to piss. One guy had the clap so bad that he could not cure it for months and had only done so with massive dosages of penicillin. His hair had turned white.

The clap sailors were charged and went to Captain's Mast where they received punishment, reductions in ranks and loss of pay. It had been the rule of the outfit. Getting the clap was in and of itself, no crime. The officers couldn't get it at all. They came down with social diseases. But if you were an enlisted man and had got the clap and had not been on R and R, then it was assumed, that you had gone out of bounds to a skivvy house, which rated a Captain Mast and disciplinary action. If you had picked up the clap on R and R, that was all right, and non-punishable, it was authorized. Such was navy justice. Only a few escaped the mast, and one of them was me. One sailor never went to mast because he rotated back to the world before the symptoms got unbearable. He never went to sick bay. He never reported that he had the clap. He took his dose back with him, to spread it around down south at church socials and in the late night back seats of old automobiles.

The liberty sailors of the Topa all had their women, and danced slowly getting excited and mashing their bodies against the young girls and one by one the couples slipped away and got by themselves.

Bear and his girl, a slim tiny teenager with a beautiful face and curvy body, thick black fox tail hair that was cut to the middle of the back and lay straight, paid the bar manager mama-san and had left the bar.

They decided on more dancing and hit a giant dance hall filled with sailors in their whites and young Filipinas colorfully dressed to entice. They danced for a while until some commotion broke out on the floor. It seemed two sailors were about to fight, amazing as it was, over a girl, or over what someone had said. It wasn't clear.

Bear and his girl moved off to the side as the crowd dispersed and tried to thin near the two potential combatants.

Just then the shore patrol burst in. Six or eight white helmeted gang busting naval police who had black SP arm bands on their whites, web belts and leggings over steel toed shoes. Their nightsticks were drawn. They waded into the potential confrontation. The sailors staring at each other never knew what hit them, never got a chance to throw a blow at one another. They were kicked, knocked down and beaten up and then summarily dragged out the door. One SP accosted a sailor who although standing close to the fray had not been involved. The SP grabbed the man's biceps. The man pulled away, exclaiming that he had not been involved. The SP jabbed his night stick as forcefully as he could into the man's face and the half drunk man, his face now bloody, slumped and then was night stick beat to the ground, and drug out the door by the helmeted military police and his buddy.

Now that the violence had been subdued, everyone went back to dance. Bear and his girl left the dance hall. They found a hotel, and paid for the little room. Bear had shelled out pesos all night, but it amounted to nothing. It had been a few pesos for the beer, a few to leave the bar, a few for the girl, a few for the dance. Now a few for the hotel room and a few more for the floor guard, who was a young muscled up Filipino, and probably put there for security. It was dingy and not well lighted place with simple accommodations, a bed with white sheets, a shower and high walls where the paint peeled off the ceiling in big leaves at the corners from the humidity.

They got naked quickly and found one another quickly in the dim light for the passionate grinding lovemaking in which Bear dominated with a violent, relieving of the tension and built up stress from so many weeks at sea. It was good to be free and alone with a woman. He was temporarily away from the power of the Navy and the ship, his surrogate mother and the evil Jg. She was laying there in the heat with the circulating fan cooling them. She looked good to him, a dark body on white sheets, with her thick full lips and almond shaped dark eyes and her thick black coarse hair sprawled on the white pillow. He reached for her and they made love again.

Doaks also sat with Filipinas, young and succulent, rubbing against his knee, and he danced and drank with them too. The beer was ice cold San Miguel, but the music was soul, and it was in an all black club. It was a segregated situation, the chucks had their place and the brothers had theirs. This cut down on a lot of violence and in Olongapo City there was plenty for everybody. It was different on the ship where the African-American was spread more or less evenly. There was more mess cooking than anywhere else. The blacks that had power on the ship, didn't get there by being no radical bloods, they got there by towing the line and doing their duty. The same as it was for everybody else. That's one thing you might give the Navy. There was a lot more racial justice inside than out. But racism was still rampant, just step out of line one time and you could see if for yourself.

Mostly it was the same for the lifers. One thing they didn't want to do is fight for it on the outside, both white and black and any other color. They were escaping nowhere jobs in nowhere places for a chance to see the world and maybe give the family chances it wouldn't have if dad was working some little gas station in South Carolina or in a steel mill in Ohio. There was no escaping the racism and or the poverty, except by heading out to sea.

In the club it was free and easy, but on the ship for Doaks the racism was not escapable. Man, he was from Chicago, he wasn't use to taking no jive from nobody especially southern chuck whites, but he had to do it or always be in trouble. So he shuffled along and did just enough to get by, barely.

Doaks had been in boot camp when they had assassinated Martin Luther King Jr., after that he didn't give a damn.

Doaks had taken his women, although she was little more than a girl, and they had gone to a nearby hotel and made love several times in the heat, their bodies glistening together in the humidity. After the last one he started beating her. It was something that she said, that infuriated him, some little thing. The thing he was pissed at wasn't her.

At the first smash the girl cried out and several muscled up Filipinos appeared at the door and swarmed all over Doaks separating him from the naked woman, knocking him to the ground, and kicked him unconscious. They threw him and his white uniform down the stairs and drug him into the street, rolling him in the mud with a long epitaph of racial slurs. The young men restrained the young women from kicking him, but not too much. She got a good one in the head and another in the kidney. Doaks groaned.

Doaks lay there in the mud and the street until the roving Shore Patrol came by and picked him up. They checked his I.D. the Dog tags he wore and his liberty card. By then he was starting to come to and they beat him up again and returned him to the ship, naked with his soiled whites in a pile. They dumped him unconscious at the foot of the prow.

"This looks like one of your boys." One of the Shore Patrol yelled up to the watch. The quarterdeck watch confiscated Doaks' liberty card and carried him below. He became sick and puked up in the head.

He crawled to his quarters took a shower as there was hot water and plenty of it and then crapped out in his rack in the Supply compartment where he was awaken at 0500 to begin the preparation of the days three chows.

Bear and Keoke stumbled back to the ship by divergent routes, drunk and satiated. Bear had had a woman and had then returned to a bar where he had drunk more and had started a brawl with an East Coaster who sneered at Oregon, throwing people around the bar until the Shore patrol rushed to the scene. He then eluded them through the streets of Olongapo, finally losing them by wading through a ditch of defecation, urine and other wastes in his whites, bare foot. He had carefully taken off his precious and rare shoes, the ones he could never get replacements for, and holding them high waded through the defecation. Once on the other side of the ditch he high tailed it for the ship. He threw away the white trousers and came aboard the Topa in his skivvy shorts, reeking of feces and urine. He walked up the gangway and passed the watch as if nothing was wrong.

Keoke had sat on the bed in the little hotel room and tried to coax the little Filipina on to his massive brown lap. His naked body gleamed with sweat and his muscles flexed and he picked up the petit women and placed her gently at his waist. He pulled her close and kissed her softly on her face then worked down to her small but exquisitely formed breasts. Keoke then lay back and she crawled on him and little by little lowering herself on him. He allowed her to move at her own speed and then began to move himself in an oval, circular motion, to the rhythm of the sea that ran through his blood. The rise and fall of the swells, the thrust and withdrawal of the tides along the reef, the slow flowing motion that was meditation, bring joy to both. She rode the rise and fall of the swell as it flowed along the reef, peeling perfectly along until it crashed all at once in the shore break exploding on the sand.

Keoke and Heavy met at the monkey meat stands outside the base and ate and talked about the night.

"Is this really monkey meat, Heavy?'

"That's what they say." Heavy said and they walked to the ship and up the gangway planks, exhausted, a little loaded but relieved.

"But it's probably dog."

They had worked out a lot of stress, and it was a good thing. Keoke had the duty the next day and couldn't go over. Bear and Semmes would be in the holds checking the cargo off load run by local Filipino stevedores. Heavy could go over to see Anna after ship work was secured.

From the 01 level in Officer's Country the Ltjg watched them come aboard, unnoticed. He was jealous.

They made it to their quarters and all passed out after crawling into the tiny racks welded to the bulkhead. I tried to sleep on the top bunk. Bear scaled the chains to his next to the top flop and stretched out scraping the aluminum rails of the bunk and shaking the whole six bunks of the tree.

Bear's feet were sticking out a foot and were only a few inches from my head. Although Bear had taken a complete shower, some of the smell from the ditch wafted up passed my nostrils and out the deck hatch which had been cracked now that we were in port. I drifted off and the next thing I heard was the mess cooks being rousted in the next row of bunk stanchions.

Doaks, after getting drunk and laid and beaten up twice was slow to make the call. He finally hit the deck, put his clothes on and staggered off toward the mess decks. Doaks knew what to do. He'd been around the block once, from the scullery to the engine room bilge to the deck. Doaks had been in the Navy for more than a year and was still a seaman apprentice. He wondered if they were ever going to let him strike for some rate. He wasn't any better off than Aqui.

The next day during ships work Bear and I found ourselves in the ship's holds, checking the offloading by the local Filipino stevedores. They were a surly bunch of bare chested muscled up, tattooed workers who wore headbands and chest scarves. We checked our own holds. The cargo went out of the hold and directly onto the pier. It didn't stop on deck. It was easy boring work, and luckily so for we were tired.

At noon chow I opened up some canned fish and took out my chop sticks I'd picked up in Taiwan and ate heartily. I was overly proud of my growing expertise with the sticks and was showing off. The Filipinos looked at me with disgust and derision. I noticed that they didn't eat with chop sticks but used their thumb and first two fingers to scoop out the rice from their lunch which were folded banana leaves containing white steamed rice and fish that was now cold.

Heavy took his chit, the one requesting permission to marry, that was all filled out and personally handed it to the Jg.

The officer took it, read it and then shook his head. The sailor was making a big mistake. He'd read all the Navy dope on why enlisted men marry local girls: Lonely, uneducated, far from home for the first time, under a lot of stress. Mostly they were marrying low class prostitutes, of little education, like themselves, and with whom they had little in common except for cheap and frequent sex. The marriages seldom lasted. It was better to discourage or somehow try to postpone, or stall, with holding permission as long as possible so as to let the love affair die a natural death. Or transfer the sailor.

"O.K. sailor, I'll take this under consideration."

"Sir, I need an answer ASAP, sir, as we'd like to..."

"All in good time, I said I'd get on it." The Jg put the chit in his khaki shirt pocket and walked down the passageway.

The same afternoon I was riding the gray walls of the narrow ship's passageways as imaginary waves when I met Aqui. I had duty and Aqui was till on restriction to the ship by the Jg.

"Why did he restrict you?" I asked furtively looking around. We were too close to Officer's Country to be talking too loud about anything important.

"He doesn't like my attitude and says I talk too much Tagalog, but the real reason is that he is restricted to the ship himself for..." Aqui lowered his voice and leaned close to my ear, "Well, he got a Social disease in Taiwan."

"What you mean, a social disease?"

"You know, he caught the clap."

"Jive me not?"

"Why would I lie, I tell you the captain's steward heard the Captain say he was restricted, and for what, till it clears up. Ask Doc." Anyway, forget that, The Jg is just pissed off. Come on up to the pantry Semmes, I got I just fried up some chicken wings and rice, you'll love it."

"Sure let's go." I said making sure my uniform and hat were squared away as I followed Aqui up the ladder to Officer's Country. We walked past the sign which proclaimed, "THIS IS OFFICER'S COUNTRY, DO YOUR OFFICIAL BUSINESS AND GET OUT!" and down the passageway to the pantry deep in Officer's Country near the wardroom.

I hung around with Aqui in the pantry and ate the delectably tender and tasty wings and rice under the "Speak English" sign, getting both my index fingers and thumbs greasy. We were done and Aqui was just washing the pan when the Jg walked in. I stiffened.

"What are you doing up here, Semmes?"

"I invited him." Aqui spoke up.

"Well you get out of here, now." The Jg said to me. I was already starting for passageway that led to freedom and down to the main deck.

"THIS IS OFFICER'S COUNTRY." He yelled after me. I could hear the Jg chewing out Aqui.

A few minutes later I saw Aqui in the Supply compartment.

"Sorry to get you in trouble." I said sheepishly, to an extremely agitated Aqui.

"He shouldn't have done that, you were my guest" Aqui said hatefully.

I patted my stomach. "At least we got to eat, thanks for the feast."

"Yeah, well the next time he lets his breakfast get cold talking up his guff in the wardroom, and wants me to warm it up, I'll be sure to cough up a nice honker and spit it on his food." We both laughed but it was interrupted by the word being passed over the squawk box.

"NOW SK3 SEMMES, LAY TO THE QUARTER DECK ON THE DOUBLE."

It was passed again.

I left Aqui and the supply compartment and laid to the Quarter Deck. The Jg was waiting for me and ordered me to report to his stateroom.

Once there the Jg. chewed me out up one side and down the other, reading me the riot act. Berating me for not running and telling me my attitude sucked. During the diatribe I stood at attention and the Jg sat down, inches from me, but at ball level.

I really didn't pay much attention but did get a look at the tiny room. I built a mental shell and only stayed alert for a question word.

There would be no more visits with my Huk friends to the wardroom pantry, ever. The Jg spit the word Filipino at me, like it was something dirty, something unclean. The Jg ended with criticism of my attitude and made the point by slamming his index finger into the bones on my chest repeatedly.

"You attitude stinks Sailor."

"Aye, Aye, sir."

"That's what I mean, put spirit in your response." The Jg screamed in my face.

"Aye, Aye, sir." I said again, but little improved, esprit de corp wise.

"Aye, aye, sir." I had learned that around the dinner table of my youth. I understand and I will obey. In this case I was not sure that I understood, nor that I would obey, but I'd been at military school, I could fake it just to get out of the officer's stateroom.

113

"Aye, aye, sir." I bellowed.

"OK sailor, dismissed." I turned around, slipped past the green curtains and down the passageway toward the main deck and out of Officer's Country.

Taking a dump later in the night, Bear felt movement in his crotch and looking down there saw a little black crab like bug scurry for cover. He caught the thing and squashed it with his fingernails and looked for more. There were none, that he could see, but he knew there were more.

He went looking for Heavy and found him high with Keoke and Reyes on the gun tub aft. Reyes and Keoke laughed, but not Heavy. He was concerned.

"Hell, Bear, if you go to sick bay, they might restrict you, the best way to cure them yourself, but you gotta do it fast. If them mothers spread from bunk to bunk all over supply, they'll probably spray us with DDT or some fool thing. OK, Keoke, get some turpentine from the paint locker. Can do?" Keoke nodded.

"Tomorrow we got day liberty, you come over to my future uncle in law's house and we will have a bath made up for you to soak in."

That night Bear picked and searched himself continually and didn't sleep in his bunk but on gun tub deck in the heat. The next day early he left with Heavy and the turpentine and went over to Heavy's future wife's extended household where Heavy mixed the tine with the hot water and had Bear get in and soak and take a bath in the stuff.

It killed all the crabs, but it also burnt Bear's skin so bad, that in some places, especially around the eyes it looked as if he had been in a terrible fight, and had lost.

"What I'm I going to do now?" Bear groaned.

"Don't worry, well go back to the ship late and hide out, by tomorrow, you'll just say you got in a hell of a fight and lost. Keoke and Reyes laughed when they saw Bear and his scares because they knew the truth, but at least Bear didn't have the crabs and neither did the Supply compartment.

It was a lazy kick back day in the Philippines and the breeze blew off the green mountains cooling down the intense tropical heat enough that "Air bedding" was ordered in the afternoon as there was no cloud burst. The bedding was hung all over the main decks and for a couple of hours the ship looked like a Chinese laundry. The offloading had been suspended and the Filipino stevedores had left the ship, and she began to top off with everything before she shoved off for the coastal Vietnam again: water, chow, and fuel.

I was perched on the chains of the bunk tree tightening the lines on my bunk when "mail call" was announced. Each division sent a rep to get the mail, then after sorting it, it was brought back to the compartment and hungrily devoured by the sailors.

I got mail so seldom that mail call being passed didn't even cause me to break my stride in pulling the rope tighter and tighter until it was taut.

"Semmes you got something." Heavy said, returning from the mail division with an arm full of letters and packages. A crowd of sailors gathered around and the mail was passed out. Heavy tossed a round brown wrapped package at me. I failed to catch it and it dropped to the deck, undamaged. I finished securing my bunk and lowered myself.

I noticed my father's writing on the expertly packed parcel. They were never damaged or hurt no matter what they went through. I opened it to find no note but a Surfer magazine. I started plastering down the cover and began paging it.

The boards were still getting smaller and smaller. They had gone from nine and ten foot to six and seven foot in just the time I'd been in the service. The year I'd been to Nam had been amazing because I'd returned to find surfers carrying eight foot boards with one hand instead of humping ten footers. It had also seemed like no one had got a haircut the whole year I was gone and the length of the whole nation's hair had seemed suddenly longer. My military haircut had set me off in a society that I had been, as a military brat, and a military school student, just a marginal participant anyway.

Coming back from Nam on the air plane we had been officially warned not to wear the uniform in public and if we were forced to, not to wear any campaign ribbons denoting service in Vietnam, because of the antiwar movement. They said that we would be targets. The thirty days at home before reporting aboard the repair ship out of San Diego were spent in lonely silence at the beach, surfing the cold waters of the California coast.

I paged the mag, in surfing the Aussies were still controlling everything and at the cutting edge. The Americans, with the exception of flashes of brilliance from the Hawaiians seemed punch drunk and only reacting to what the Aussies did. The girls in the mag were skimpily dressed and blonde. They were no more than an illusion, at least until I could get out and melt into civilian society. If that was possible! The surf spots displayed, some foreign, some home, were also out of reach, just like the glossy new boards displayed on the glossy pages.

It had been fine on the repair ship. It was jokingly called an extension of pier thirteen. It rarely went to sea. It had been easy to get standbys for the daily surf and half a day off on rope yarn Wednesday when he and Jay would either go north to surf Trestles on the marine base or south across the border to K-55.

Rope yarn Wednesday was coming to the office in whites in preparation for early liberty at 1200 and then dashing to the vans, one day we'd take mine, one day we'd take Jay's, and then the run up or down the coast for the surf. Riding almost every day the San Diego summer surf and jetting home to Ventura for the weekends was a good niche to get into. I was happy as I could be in the Navy and in good shape. Since the girls in the bikinis were out of reach, the concentration was on the surf.

The others stood around and read their mail or sat on the bottom bunk rail, some sprawled on the deck. Some left to be alone.

"Oh." somebody said, "my girl is dating some old dude."

"My old girl's going with some college student."

"My old girl friend married my best buddy on leave." another said.

"Maybe your girl will learn something." Somebody smirked.

"You say one more word and I'm going to beat your ass."

"You can try right now." The other said as they both flinched for combat.

"You two knock it off." A second class said.

"He's making fun of me, my girl is going out with some dude who is twenty-six she met at college." Everybody laughed.

"At least she ain't going out with the whole fleet like Bird's woman."

"That ain't true," Bird interjected. "When I'm not home she only goes out with marines.

"Oh, yeah, you forgetting that fleet support medal she got."

"Wow" I exclaimed. My head still buried deep in Surfer Magazine.

"Look at that shape, the fine lines,"

Everyone gather around me expecting to see a nice looking babe. All they saw was a white surfboard displayed on the dark page.

"Beautiful, isn't she. I bet she's fast." I murmured, obviously infatuated with the surfboard.

"Semmes, you out of your frigging mind."

"I did some surfing before." Somebody said. "I rented one of them there surfboards at Waikiki."

"Semmes, when you get out of the Navy, are you going to quit surfing and become respectable?" I just smiled.

The story was interrupted by the static of the squawk box.

"NOW SK3 SEMMES LAY TO THE X.O.'S OFFICE ON THE DOUBLE."

The message was repeated and everybody murmured.

"What now, Semmes?" Heavy asked, his eyes jerked up.

"Semmes's on the most wanted list, everybody want to rap with him."

"Who knows?" I said immediately leaving the group and unconsciously checking myself to see if I was squared away, tucking in my shirt and polishing my shoes on my dungaree pants, making my way to the main deck and then to Officer's Country.

Once in Officer's Country going toward the Executive Officer's office, I saw the Jg in the narrow passageway.

"What kinda trouble you in now, Sailor." I didn't know either. It was none of the Jg's doings for a change. I shrugged an answer. The Jg shot me a contemptuous stare, but let me proceed. I knocked loud enough to be heard but as submissively as possible on the Executive's Officer's office door. It was opened and the X.O. stood in front of me, towering over me.

"Someone wants to talk to you sailor, you better cooperate." The X.O. said and then slipped down the passageway toward the wardroom panty.

"Aye, sir." I said to the departing figure. I knocked on the door and went in. There was a man in a tropical suit and a flowered shirt that bade me to sit. The man introduced himself as ONI, Office of Naval Intelligence. A contradiction in terms I thought. The man proffered a card to me, which I took and read carefully. The I.D. card did indeed say Office of Naval Intelligence. I tried to think what thing I'd done wrong.

"We'd like to ask you a couple of question about one of your former shipmates." I glanced around to see if someone else was in the room. The guy meant him and the agency. The man had been pausing for effect but it was lost on me.

"Jay Budd." he said.

Jay was a big surfer dude from the San Fernando Valley, the guy who I rode with while we had both been stationed on the repair ship in San Diego. We knew each other from "A" school. I didn't find out until later that Big Jay had written a letter to a friend, also in the Navy that had said: "We are getting high on the surf, I hear there is some good acid going around." Budd had signed the letter with a peace sign. The addressee sailor had gone over the hill, had been AWOL and his locker had been searched. When the incriminating letter had been found it was passed to the proper authorities. ONI. They had checked with the ship's officers and had found out Jay and I had gone on liberty together. They were also investigating Jay, who on his ship, was also deployed in the West Pac area.

I looked at the man.

"Has something happened to Jay?"

"He's in a lot of trouble, sailor." At least they had stopped calling me lad. The man lied. Actually, ONI had confronted Jay with the evidence, the letter, but Jay had gotten a good lawyer, a marine to represent him. The flimsy accusation was still pending. Looking up his old shipmates, ONI was trying to get some corroborating evidence. Evidence that Jay used drugs, or that he was a subversive, a peace freak.

"Let's see, you served with Jay from the time you got back from Vietnam until you were transferred here and went on liberty with him many times, didn't you?"

"Yes Sir." I said truthfully, realizing that this man wanted me to somehow incriminate Jay, and maybe myself too.

"Where did you go on Liberty?"

"First, we just hit the area around San Diego proper, but then we started to ride almost exclusively North County San Diego, except for rope yard Wednesdays, then we'd either go north, to The Trestles or south to Mexico."

"Why did you go there, to North County, for example?"

"Well San Diego is really good on a south swell, as long as it's not too south, we usually hit the place, say Solana or other beach breaks around glass off. All the kids would be home for evening chow and it would be glassing off, you know, real smooth, and not crowded and Jay and I would get really good waves. After we'd ride, we'd chow some place and then come back to the ship." I neglected to tell the man that we'd be tired but happy and ready to commence ship's work the next day.

"Did you ever meet anyone there?

"No, it's too hard to meet people, they know right off we're Navy and stay away from us, especially in Dago, especially the girls. We did surf Trestles this one time, that's up at the Marine base, Camp Pendleton, it was low incoming tide and the waves were about five foot with bigger sets. We paddled out and I saw Jay get completely tubed twice in one wave. I mean covered up. Anyway, we were surfing when the marines came down to kick everybody out of the water, there were two other guys surfing there. They got chased away, but the jar head Lt. said we could go back and surf. Jay explained to him we'd been to Nam and such.

"Tell me about Mexico." The man said smiling.

"Well we usually hit this place called K55, nice little lined up beach break, warm water, no crowds. I remember we got it this day. It was probably three to four feet, but one of those days when the water is so clean and the shape was excellent. You could see the sand ripples on the bottom. That day Jay got really far back in the tube. I could see him clear as anything, through the back of the wave.

"Did Jay ever talk about drugs?"

"Yes Sir." I said and the man brightened. Now he was getting somewhere.

"What did he say?"

"He said that people who used drugs were crazy and that they were ruining their health. You have to be healthy and in shape to surf. I remember when he said that cause we were surfing Swami's, that's in the north county, on a good south swell. It wasn't wrapping off the outside point like it does on a big north, but it sure was pretty inside. The tide had just maxed out and so the waves were optimum size if a little slow. I had just taken off on the pretty good face and.

"OK, OK. Did he ever talk politics?"

"Not that I remember, but I do remember we were pulling off some good tubes just north of Cardiff Reef, it was one of those low tide days, you have to take off quick, duck in and get covered up...."

"OK, OK." The ONI man looked a little frustrated with the surf filibuster. Man was looking for information, but all he was getting was surf story. He could barely understand what I was talking about. He tried again after all there was still the peace sign.

"Did Jay ever say he was against the war in Vietnam?" To me it did seem like a strange question. After all Jay and I had served there. How could someone who'd been there and saw it and was part of the madness been anything but against the war? But I was smart enough not to say much. Actually, we had never discussed it. I would think about it in the distant future.

"Jay was pissed about being in Saigon and having to live in that hotel with the Nav Sup when we were up in Da Nang getting some surf when we worked nights and could go after work and get some day waves. All he had was a skateboard and the roof of the hotel. We were riding Velzy pop outs the Aussies had brought into Nam."

"One last question, do you know what political party Jay belonged to?"

I tried to think of who was president, that year it was peace with honor Nixon. 68' had been his first election. When I had gone to register the officer had asked me why I had wanted to vote, and all I could think of to say was, "It's my right, sir."

"I think he said he was a Republican, sir." The officer shook his head and excused me from the interrogation. The officer of Naval Intelligence left the ship a short while later without any evidence against some storekeeper second class, also ten thousand miles away from home, who had written a letter to a fellow sailor who had gone over the hill.

When I returned to the compartment and told the tale, Keoke said, "You messed up, little haole bra, you should have told them, of course you and your buddy get high. You get high, so very high off the kelp and the surf and the ocean, and dats mo better than any drug, and that's the only reason you joined the Navy in the first place was to get paid for getting high. You really messed up, you had your chance and you lost it."

It was something for me to think about.

After one port and one starboard liberty, liberty was secured for me at night. A few days later everyone was restricted. So if you didn't make it on the first or second day, you were out of luck.

Aqui didn't get to go over.

Reyes never made his phone call to Alison.

Topa tied up to a new fast supply and support ship for transshipment of cargo. Topa worked around the clock, only eating and sleeping to finish the job.

I did get off the ship on a hot and humid day. The old gray girl just sat there in its' own stench and sweat, buzzing and droning and humming. Clouds of silver whiteness began forming against a deep blue sky. Later in the afternoon, they would burst with violence and cleanse the earth. The sun glittered brightly off the puddles and the ditches and made it difficult to see. My Dixie cup white sailor hat was no protection against the tropical sun. I kept my head down, watching my white pants and black shoes step along the road. They carefully sidestepped all the puddles.

There was precious little I wanted to see until the money changes at the base gate were all behind me, until the ship and the base and the officers were all behind me. The loading was almost over and this was probably going to be the last liberty I would get in the P.I. Perhaps there would be a little for the lucky half of the crew for a few hours just before we pulled out.

Day liberty was a different experience, since the bars weren't full of drunken sailors and since I had the morning to myself, there weren't going to be any fights or shore patrol cracking heads. No bottle smashed in your face or a chair busted over your head or back.

I walked a little down the street and ducked in a bar. I stood just inside the door and waited for my eyes to adjust to the dimmer surroundings. A long black mahogany bar lay in front of me. Empty tables were to my right. I was almost alone in the place. At the other end, near the kitchen door a mama san sat on what looked like a high chair. We smiled at each other long distance. Turning her head she uttered something abruptly while I reached for a stool and sat at the bar. A fresh wet breeze blew through the bar, cooling my already sweating body. I took off my white hat and folding it, stuck it into my pants on the same side I usually wore my keys. The mama san waddled toward me from the side of the bar and with her wrinkled dark almond eyes asked me my pleasure. I ordered a San Miguel.

A girl came up to me and put one arm around my waist and the other she placed gently on my forearm which was sprawled across the bar.

"Hi." she smiled at me with a flawless white smile and a perfect dark complexion.

"What's your name?"

"Stores." I said, "People call me stores."

"I know you storekeeper, here cross keys, but what's your name?" she asked running her soft hand along my third class crow. Her hands curled around my biceps which held the cross keys below the eagle. The eagle that looked like it had just landed or was about to take flight, its wings flung out trying to feel the air currents.

"What real name?" Her eyes narrowed and pleaded into mine. I had to think for a minute. Nobody ever called me by my first name. It was either stores or Semmes or the hated tag 'sailor,' which sometimes could start a fight. I thought about my shipmates and realized I knew no first names, except Keoke's. I looked into her black pools and said.

"Steven." It sounded strange and unfamiliar to me. "What's your name?"

"Baby" she said, and she was a baby.

"You buy Baby a drink?" I ordered her a drink. We both knew that it was just colored water, very expensive colored water. It was how the bars made even more money. I asked for another beer and Baby's long black hair brushed against my arm and it send tinkles through my body, as she got off the stool and went around to the back of the bar to get another ice cold San Miguel. I watched her strong legs disappear around the bar, then return. Her eyes approached again smiling, her hands holding out an ice cold San Miguel. She was offering the bottle to me. I laid some pesos on the bar and looked back into her ebony eyes.

"You're beautiful." I told her. She smiled back at me.

"You're beautiful too." She said. I could smell her perfume and it intoxicated me. I wondered how young she was. I was a lot older than she was. I was pushing twenty-two.

The little girl and I were a lot alike. We didn't have our own lives. Both were at the bidding of others, those stronger and more powerful. She was just beginning. I could see myself getting away from it. I would get away from the Navy if I didn't become entangled, in debt, or put in the brig. And I would get out if when the time came I had the strength to walk away, to get the separation papers and walk away.

She was laughing and whispering in my ear. I had to keep bending over closer and closer to hear her better. Now she had her arm around my neck and I had my arm around her small waist. She had prior permission from Mama-san. She told me we could leave and in a swig I finished my beer, the residue, and the dregs, already hot like the tropics. Mama-san collected the money with a blank look on her face. She folded the money and put it in her pocket.

We left the bar and ventured into the streets, hand in hand but I followed her. The sun was just now overhead blazing upon us. We didn't walk far on the narrow sidewalk when she entered a hotel she knew and everyone knew her. In this she was safe. I paid the man at the front desk for a room. She led me up the stairs to the second floor and down the wide hall. A solitary Filipino dozed, guarding at the end of the hall, just in case, just in case somebody got violent. It was too early and there was no business. That would come later when the ships in Subic went on liberty.

I kissed her right off and she backed away from me. I put my hand behind my back and leaned down and kissed her without fondling her. She hesitated then kissed me around the mouth and neck. She reached her hands high around my neck and we moved closer together.

I cupped her small but broad breasts. When she was older they were going to be massive, now they were just starting to swell with her young age. I could feel myself moving inside of her tightness, in excruciating joy. Later, we watched the overhead fan twirl and the shadows from the lowering sun breaking high on the wall. Baby, had her thick raven hair flung across my chest, put her head up and then she slapped my flat stomach.

"Time to go?" she said. I laughed and tried to turn her over but she broke away. I caught her and forced her down and kissed her again. I looked closely into her eyes then caressed her again.

We both smiled and laughed. We felt the tropic heat and heard the growing number of sailors on the streets of the port city. I had to get back to the ship. I knew that I had added to the exploitation of the Filipino people by taking this young girl, but in another way we were both on the same turf. She'd go back to the bar and hustle drinks and sailors and I'd go on the ship, and it would go a whoring along the coast of Vietnam. Neither could say no, except under the greatest consequences. We got up and took a shower, the water cooling us and covering us in the humidity. We moved swiftly, washing our bodies and preparing our minds to return to what reality we knew. Nothing much was said as we caressed and lathered each other up. We dressed and left the room moving down the hall and then down the dimly lighted stairs.

The artificial light hit us like reflections from church stained glass. We emerged on the streets that were beginning to pulsate and seethe with activity of the lost souls.

We kissed in a last caress, and then left each other, returning to our separate stations, losing ourselves in the crowd and losing each other.

I had just come back off liberty, my body still alive with fever, when a second group of sailors were given liberty. The loading operations had just finished at 1700, and liberty was granted from 1800 to 2100 and then the ship was to pull out. The captain wanted to get back to the combat zone off Vietnam so he could get his combat pay. That's why the short liberty.

The men had worked hard, and were in such a bad mood that they didn't even try for any women. They went into the first bar and ordered beers and drank them quickly, mumbling. Soon they were drunk and pissed and didn't care anymore. Someone threw a bottle and it broke against the wall. Then another was thrown and it broke and there was a cheer. Another sailor stood up and broke a chair over the table. They weren't fighting each other. They were purging their rage. They were breaking up the bar.

The owners called the Shore Patrol. Heavy and Reyes were just leaving when the SP's barreled into the place and began breaking heads. Bear, drunk and oblivious to their presence sat there trying to bust a glass San Miguel beer on the table. He looked up at the Shore Patrol, and grinned at them, laughing softly, and then he lunged at them as they waded toward him through the litter on the deck.

Keoke jumped in against the SP's but with reinforcements, they finally subdued the men and beat them up and took them back to dump them on the ship.

Others came back to the ship, drunk and bleeding, crawled into their racks to sleep it off.

A few minutes after 2100 we were called to muster on deck. It took us a little longer time to get there than it normally would have. The Jg appeared in the supply compartment screaming and yelling for us to muster on the main deck hatch square. It was dangerous for him to be there alone after dark. He heard the drunken men in their cramped little bunks curse him and the Navy. He retreated as they stumbled on deck.

It seems there were some pallets still on the ship. The drunken sailors formed a working party and got the job done quickly.

We then were mustered and bitched out by the Jg., who had probably been bitched out by the Commander or the Captain. He jumped up on the hatch's square cover and started to be-little us. It was night and at least half the sailors were pissed and drunk. The hated officer was in front of them.

Bear had had enough and lunged at the officer but I caught and restrained him, pushing him back. The Jg looked terrified and said some cursory remarks then retreated to the 01 level of Officer's Country, after dismissing the men. Bear and I were locked in an obscene dance for a few seconds as the Jg got away, and Bear grumbled drunkenly.

"Let me at um, I'll kill um." He mumbled over and over again. I helped Bear below decks and the men left alone, the work done, calmed down and became quiet.

The ship, the tired old Topa just about on her last leg, pulled out for the transit across the South China Sea to the coast of Vietnam. She was ready for another go at underway replenishment as part of task force 73 of the U.S. Seventh Fleet.

CHAPTER 7

Deployment: Dixie Station, South China Sea, Gulf of Siam

The ship steamed for the coast of Vietnam with a brown spot from all the sailors who had diarrhea trailing her. Doc, in the aft sick bay was a harried, balding second class corpsman. What they used to call a pharmacist mate. He was busy distributing medicine that would stop the runs and preparing for the clap cases that were sure to emerge after a stay in any liberty port. Doc thanked God he was not with the FMF, the Fleet Marine Force, and was glad all he had to worry about was clap and diarrhea, colds and the odd minor injury, maybe a case of the crabs. He knew that if he was with the fleet marine, like a lot of his class mates from "A" school, he'd be taking live rounds while working on dying jar heads in the mud, and maybe dying himself. Enough of his classmates had been wounded or killed already, so he realized how lucky he was not to be in country in Vietnam. Approaching its coast though, he had to think about it.

As the ship headed to make its run on the coast to re supply and replenish in the summer of 1969 the constant struggle at home for college campuses had ended for the summer, but the antiwar students were preparing for an active fall. National moratoriums would begin October 15th. By that time Ho Chi-minh would be dead. Nixon had ordered secret bombings of Cambodia. The Phoenix Assassination program was in full swing. In Paris, Kissinger met surreptitiously with Vietnamese Communists. Nixon would soon announce the Vietnamization of the war and token troop withdrawals. Fathers Barrigan would be convicted for antiwar activities, namely destroying draft records, burning them with napalm. Neil Armstrong would, with other Americans would land on the moon. Woodstock would happen in New York State and actress Sharon Tate would be killed in a cult slaying.

My Lai, still being covered up by officers of the Americal Division, would break into the news later in the year. Two hundred and forty two Americans were killed in one week and a magazine ran all their photos. The miracle Mets were rolling toward a pennant and World Series victory.

In 1969, they were dying like flies, both Vietnamese and Americans in the Ashau Valley, Hamburger Hill and elsewhere.

On the Topa, steaming Yankee station north and Dixie station south, underway replenishment continued, day in and day out with nonchalance. The ships would appear from dawn till dusk, hundreds of feet away from the Topa, and at near full power runs and get what they wanted. She ran as far south as An Thoi on Phu Quoc Island in the Gulf Of Siam, and resupplied LSTs at the mouth of the Bassac River in the Mekong Delta and supplied all types of craft, destroyers, mine sweepers, hospital ships, and large and small shore facilities that she could get to or could get to her.

If the war was being wound down, the men couldn't tell.

Bear started screaming in the head one early morning before unrep. I stepped in to see him gripping on to the urinal pipes. His urine track was plugged due to the clap.

"What's going on Bear?" Heavy asked.

"Man, its hurts when I piss hurts, hurts.

"Go see Doc, and he'll fix you up."

"Yeah, maybe, although I seen some cases in Nam they couldn't do anything with." I said.

"Shut up Semmes, ain't no way to talk."

Later in the sick bay Bear asked Doc.

"Will I go blind?" Doc laughed.

"I hope not. It's only the clap. I'll give you some penicillin." Bear prepared himself for the shots, looking away from his arm, relaxed.

"This and the pills I'm giving you will knock it out. Too bad I can't do anything with those feet." The Doc said.

"Leave my feet alone Doc, they might look big here but in the mill back in Oregon, I do the work easier. Other guys had to move their feet. I just had to pivot on my heel to change those gears. Boss told me I always had a job there." They laughed. Bear left and returned to the compartment thinking of how good it would be to be home again, drinking beer and getting rowdy and putting in his forty hours at the mill.

Reyes and a snipe were looking at the outer bulkhead, of the Supply Compartment scratching their chins and hemming and hawing.

"Yeah," Reyes said. "Must have been right here."

"Shore enough, look at these stress cracks along this beam here. Right along here she must have parted."

"What? What?" Heavy and others said, suddenly interested. "What broke up?"

Reyes turned to face them.

"Topa's sister ship off Norfolk, in a storm." He ran his hand along the gray surface that kept them from the sea, shaking his head in a negative manner.

"Talk about something else." Jake half ordered.

"We don't got to worry about it, surfer boy Semmes here will show us how to ride the wild surf." Bear said and everybody guffawed.

"If it comes down, I'm grabbing one of your shoes, Bear, but I'll need some you other swabbies to help me handle it." There were more chuckles.

"Hey Semmes, what did your Dad do in California? Sell surfboards and rent umbrellas at the beach?"

"Well, ah, he was a chief boatswain mate."

"In the U.S. Navy?" Doaks asked around the corner. "Hey fellows come here, these chiefs, actually got families and stuff."

"Well how was it growing up with a chief?"

I hesitated then played it up.

"It wasn't no different that you all growing up, except when I joined the Navy I just got a transfer." There were smirks and looks of half credence and half disbelief. I continued.

"The other stuff was the same, me and my brother on port and starboard watches, pipe my Dad aboard, reveille at 0600, taps at 2200, lucky to stay in any place very long." I trailed off.

"Then you're not really a Californian, I mean born?" Bear said.

"Naw, I was born in Norfolk, Virginia."

"Well, that is something for you."

"Damn, old shit city, old Nafock."

"We were transferred to Dago when I was young." Other low ranking enlisted men gather around to hear the stories about how it was growing up with a Chief boatswain, on Navy bases with glee and disbelief. Then they were all called away to general quarters and every one scurried away to their appropriate stations.

It was a beautiful day on the South China Sea, blue, clear, with flying fish jumping off the bow wake and the ships wake white against the blue sea. There wasn't an unrep in sight so the old man spent the whole day in drills, GQ, Abandon ship, and damage control. Mostly I waited at GQ in the heat and sweated. It was better than being in the hold.

Bear was on the bridge when an officer asked him how many people were taking fixes. Bear thought for a minute and asked the officer.

"Sir, do you mean here on the ship or back in San Francisco?" The officer looked at him aghast.

"Navigational fixes, sailor, Navigational fixes." Bear turned red and said he didn't know. The officer looked at him and shook his head in disbelief. Maybe there was a drug problem on board.

On the bow, me, the Chief Master at Arms and a lifer first class shared the fire control station in the open observational just above the guns, tracking imaginary targets that the bridge would alert them to.

The system was designed during the Second World War for the three man crew to spot the target, and then lock the gun onto it and control the firing. The gun could also be fired manually by the gun crew. And that's how it was always done. The three storekeepers at the fire control had never, nor would they ever really fire the guns. So there we languished, and during live firing, had a great view of the gun crew. If there was a misfire or hang fire and an explosion ensued, or the gun was actually hit we would all be dead.

When we were not directly involved I tracked what was available, a bird, a flying fish, some dolphins.

The wind blew freshly off the bow, even in a calm sea as the Topa plowed through at 12 knots. I loved the sea almost as much as I disliked the Navy. I had grown up around both and found something that was sea but was not navy and that was surfing. I might have been in a better mind chipping paint on the deck force and standing underway watches but my dad had ordered me clearly.

"Don't be a deck ape like me. Learn something in the Navy you can use on the outside. Take a gunner's mate for example. How many civilian employers have five inch guns?" Try to be a yeoman or a personnel man or a storekeeper. If you want to go career, the army or the Air force is the best. Then you can take your family with you. You can't do that on a ship."

I remembered the ship coming back, my father on the bow with the first Lieutenant.

Once the Bosun was home there was a change of command in the family as the softness of the mother was changed back to the Navy way. The home was like the Navy. My dad sang reveille to get us up in the morning.

"I can't get them up,
I can't get them up,
I can't get them up in the morning,
I can't get um up,
I can't get um up,
I can get up in the m-o-r-n."

He called us for chow.

"Come and get your chow, boys.
Come and get your chow.
Come and get your chow, boys
Come and get your chow."

There was a plan of the day, ship's work, then when done, we could `Shove off for liberty.' The metal gray of the gun deck and the fire control station and the blue China Sea brought it all back. The Navy reminded me of home.

When I thought of home, I got images of the sea grass covered dunes overlooking the Atlantic or identical gray cracker box houses set on cliffs above the Pacific and then gray Quonset hut school rooms set in flat open grass covered fields. Bases and ships and gray and blues, and little bone Buddhas on the mantle, of getting orders, and packing and going to another port or duty station. The Navy was home. Home was the Navy.

Later on the mess decks, the Yeoman had an idea. He would try to get music set up for the crew to listen to during chow. All the different parts of the crew had their own music. The African Americans had soul, the white city boys had rock and roll, the red necks liked country and western, and there were some few scattered among the rest who liked Jazz, folk and classical. That's what the yeoman liked, classical. If everybody put in some representative examples of their music the crew could listen to music during chow and this would sooth them and calm them down.

The idea spread like excited scurvy fire through the crew infecting everybody. The Yeoman had put a tape player he had bought in Taiwan on the mess decks and had the electricians hook up a sound system. All the different factions submitted their music to him. People were seen approaching him with tapes and albums they had from their collections, their favorites. Then everyone waited and expectations rose among each group. The tape deck was readied, and one morning at sea the crew came to the mess decks for chow and ate to music, country music.

For those who like country and western, it was pure pleasure. All the blacks, and the white boys from the city hated it but they figured they could handle it. After all they had all submitted their music too.

Doaks sitting on the pier in Alameda had had a soul playing radio tossed in to the bay. Different types of music might have soothed their fans but they seemed to infuriate others.

The men on the mess decks waited and bided their time. Doaks was mess cooking, and was constantly hot and sweaty in the scullery. He would be up before the crew's reveille by more than an hour and would knock off well after the crew's mess at night. There was morning chow, noon chow and evening chow and mid rats for those on watch. There was breaking out the chow for the next day's meals and washing all the cups, glasses, plates, trays and all the silver ware in the intense heat of the scullery. There were also the big kettles and pots and pans to be scrubbed in a constant fury of work.

The galley fed two hundred men three times a day and that was a lot of washing dishes and pots, pans and kettles. His hands were constantly cut and had open sores that were bleached white on the rims with dead skin but swollen red at the apex of the cuts. For the really bad cuts he had learned just to tape them, not use a bandage and leave them on. Doaks had been working the scullery for a long time and there seemed no end in sight.

The mess cooks only broke for GQ and UNREP. Sometimes they had some time off between meals, except that the cook, Mr. Jekyll, hated blacks and kept Doaks doing nothing just to keep him busy, cleaning the bulk heads in the office or the storeroom or the mess decks or the galley.

The music from the mess decks seeped in to his scullery area through the square entrance where the crew left their trays when they were done eating. He made a face as the music penetrated his ears. It was all the things he hated, all the things that caused him trouble, some white chuck music. At best it reminded him of the blues his dad listened to when Doaks was a little boy.

The morning chow had country music. At noon there was country. Many were disappointed that there had been no change. It would have been only fair to rotate, like the watches. At dinner, the frustrated sailors heard country again. The crew figured the music would be rotated on a daily basis and waited for the morning chow for a substantive change. The next morning, there was no change and the crew was greeted with wild fiddles and guitars of a rousing country tune.

Doaks had had enough, and took off the scullery white hat and threw down his plastic apron. He came out of the scullery doing a hoe down dance, kicking up his heels and giving a rebel yell. Everyone turned and watched Doaks strut among the mess deck tables. He let out another long rebel yell and went into a deep squat like a Cossack, now kicking his feet above his head with acrobatic acumen. Everybody, maybe especially the red neck country boys caught the fever and started to whistle and stomp and clap their hands to the beat of the music and Doaks' gyrations. The mess decks reverberated with thundering howling and hooting.

It didn't take long for the chiefs and one officer to arrive on the scene to quell and quiet the men down. As soon as the officer entered the room it became quiet. The music was summarily turned off and the tape deck and the speakers were removed from the mess decks that morning while the men ate and no one spoke of having music on the mess decks during chow for the crew ever again.

The Topa steamed in the South China Sea, the crew exhausted and bored by the endless days with little water and poor food. That day for a finale, before going off the line they had unrepped a big wooden deck cruiser who had skivvy waved over a question.

"Our guns our eight inch, how big are your?' The skivvy wavers on the Topa replied.

"Our West Pacs are six months, how long are yours?" This shut them up because they did duty for about nine. The cruiser had such a large compliment of men that they had a band playing on the 0 something level amidships which the sailors on the Topa could easily hear, since it wasn't far away, during unrep. The ships had broken off and Topa secured from the unrep detail, the hatches were closed and the scuttlebutt was that the ship was heading north for Hong Kong. Half the crew believed it and half disbelieved, but everybody hoped it was so. Rumors sped through the ship like wild fire pushed by a hot Santa Ana wind in dry chaparral, and changed more often than the deck and engineering's rotating watches.

I had crapped out on the deck aft where the five inch gun mount had been removed in the nineteen fifties. I lay on a deck that was still warm from the tropic heat that had beat down on it all day, every day, as a primitive use of solar power. I looked up at the stars in the sky, billions and billions of tiny white lights that rolled above him spreading almost from horizon to horizon across the sky.

I had developed a knack for sleeping anywhere. I had slept through the landings and takeoffs as a baby in Virginia without even a stir, so my father had said. Working in the fields with the Mexicans as a teenager home from military school I had crawled down underneath the truck on to the dirt of the Oxnard Plain and napped before the harsh, "Vamos a trabajar" of the bosses woke me up after lunch. In Nam I'd slept on thousand pound bombs and among stacks of 155 rounds and in the holds of LSTs which loaded and unloaded their cargoes at Tien Sha ramp. The roar of the rough terrain fork trucks, announcing that the off load was beginning again would wake me up.

Now I felt myself unable to doze off. Perhaps I was too tired to sleep or too wired from coffee or too excited about going to Hong Kong, if the rumors were true. First my mind was back in California riding long point break waves on my mini gun with a big fin. I'd buy a new board when I got back. I'd go to the Ventura surf shop this time. The board I'd bought, the one the Jg had let go in Keelung harbor had been from the best surf board maker in Santa Barbara. I'd gone right to the shop on State Street and picked out the board from a window display. It had been a pintail and they'd looked at me like I was crazy, like I was a stupid squid, a dumb swabbie spending money like a sailor on leave. Money to burn. Money saved from the one hundred and sixty a month I made in Nam as a seaman making combat pay. What a board it was. I thought of my new board and imagined myself riding the cool glassy waves of home.

I thought about my Mom and Dad's military marriage and could see just how strong those people were. Thinking of the things they had endured and had never complained about, the long absences from their families, the crummy housing and the groveling to the officers and their wives. Race had never been much of a question to me, but the officer and enlisted bar was.

"You can't play with Johnny any more, you know his dad's an officer." I thought of officer's wives who'd refused to be interviewed by or to interview enlisted men's wives during the census. It was way below their dignity. I imagined my father taking guff from the officers for more than twenty years, and unlike them with their college degrees, he had few career options to fall back on when the Navy time ended. So my father and mother had hung in there and had taken the guff, did what they were told, moved their families all around the country or left us in some port town during deployment. All this so we could have a better chance at it. And where was I now? My parents had made incredible sacrifices, even for someone like my father, and myself who loved the sea and the ship although I could barely admit it to myself and never spoke of it to another.

In the distance among the sounds of the sea, water rushed against the ship. I felt the tug of the wind, gusting and backing off again. Among the occasional smell of the smoke stack pollution and the constant and reassuring buzz of the ship, I heard someone ascending the ladder to the abandoned gun tub. At first I stiffened, then relaxed when I realized at this late hour it would not be an officer. They never came on deck at night, especially the aft main deck where they were cut off by the crew's quarters from the Officer's Country of the super structure. The figure appeared, a ball cap and in the dark, dungaree pants and a white t-shirt in the black night. It was Reyes.

"Semmes, I been looking for your worthless, raggedy ass."

"What's up?"

"Let's go smoke a number." Reyes said. "Let's go to the high point of the ship." We left the gun tub and walked forward to the super structure, then climbed up the ship's ladders past the Officer's Country then up the ships mast in the black night as far up as we could go. We were high and all that was below us was the dark sea and the white wake cutting behind the ship. Above were the radars and a blanket of stars. The warm wet tropical wind whipped our short hair and clothes around frantically. We were sitting as high as we could go on the mast. Reyes produced a joint and with his zippo lighter put a flame to it taking a deep hit and passing it to me. I cupped it and took a deep hit. We continued smoking and passing the joint back and forth to the roll of the ship, and all the while losing big whiffs of the smoke to the endless sea.

"It is like our lives." Reyes said sitting there feeling the effects of the weed.

"What is?" I asked.

"The smoke we lost to the wind. We're just wasting our lives here." The wind rattled the guy wires and lines and the radar kept turning and the ship buzzed on toward Hong Kong. We could feel the ship roll and the wind gust.

Semmes thought of the surf he was going to ride when he got out. Reyes thought of his wife. He got the feeling something wasn't right. There was nothing either one could do about it, they could just sit back and enjoy the high and try to stay out of trouble until there was something they could do about it.

Reyes, because he was more from the world, more of a civilian, knew better that this military time was dead time. The barrio was changing, and people were going to school and working and getting educated and experienced while they languished in a lost cause, on an old ship, in the South China Sea. Reyes knew they were being left behind and that they were never going to catch up. Their peers would have too much of a jump on them.

The next stop was Hong Kong. Heavy would pick up some dope there. The ship's five thousand tons of cargo wouldn't last forever. Plus the old girls engines were weak. Soon they'd be homeward bound. Homeward bound and freedom bound.

"Let's get outta here."

"Look!" I whispered and pointed down to the 0-1 level near the boat deck. It was the Jg. and he was taking his kind of constitutional, standing at the rail and looking out to sea.

We watched him, with hate, perched above him for once. After ten minutes there Jg returned to Officer's Country.

"It's right there he clubbed Tecolote, Do you remember?"

I shook my head. It seemed like a long time ago. Reyes and I scurried carefully down the ladders and made our way to our own bunks, behind the superstructure and below the main deck. Once we lay on our bunks sleep came easy. Fantasies churned in our minds, of perfect waves and pretty women, and fantasies about how to off the Jg.

The ship pulled through the narrow passage and into Hong Kong harbor and found herself among the hustling bustling waters. Junks and sampans, lighters, cargo ships and ferries crowded everywhere. Hong Kong was surrounded by hills, like those of San Francisco, but steeper. Hong Kong was an open port, a free port and China's, gateway to the world. British owned, and run, if almost all the residents were Chinese. China with a tiny, tiny European fringe but China, never the less.

The men were restricted from going on deck unless they had undress whites on. This was to show the ships friendly intent. After a few minutes of silent rebellion the crew, little by little, went down into the compartment and changed into whites and came on deck to see the port of Hong Kong. Its pull was stronger than the hate and defiance they felt for the Navy, or the officers.

Ships from every country plied the waters of the harbor. A large Red Chinese junk, with the red sickle and hammer flag motored past as the ship moored at the second buoy in Honk Kong harbor.

The crew was mustered on the deck and was advised, by the Jg. not to buy anything made in Red China. They were warned to stay away from the Wanchai district, and told that if they happened to find themselves there, not to go above the first floor. This was a part of Hong Kong with a lot of Communist activity.

The ship had just moored when Mary Soo's motorized sampan came out from shore and approached the accommodation ladder, which had just been lowered to the water. The little vessel had Mary Soo and her first Lieutenant in the stern sheets. They were both stately looking middle aged Chinese women of great dignity and carriage. There was a faded flag on the little craft slightly jumping in the breeze that, on its old and faded surface, had the Topa's name and number.

They came along side and one of the men in the boat, the bow hook, held the accommodation ladder steady so the women could board, as the small engine idled.

The Jg had the deck and at first he tried to shout the little vessel away, warning it with ugly snarling and verbal intimidation. The Chinese women paid no attention to him and boarded the ladder and began a slow ascent to the Jg's deck watch position. The P.O. of the watch, Reyes said nothing, although he knew Mary Soo. Who could tell the Jg anything?

Now the Jg, being ignored by the approaching Chinese women, was livid and began to threaten. The women continued to make slow but steady and stately progress toward the in port quarterdeck. The Jg began screaming for them to halt, and he unbuttoned the holster on his hip that had the 45 caliber automatic pistol. Reyes was trying to decide whether or not he was going to intervene if the Jg was crazy enough to pull the side arm. Reyes looked aloft beseechingly, even religiously for help from any senior officer. He needed help from somebody who knew what the hell was going on. The Captain, from the wing of the bridge, observing all, as a god will, finally intervened.

"Jg, escort that woman to the bridge." The Jg's mouth dropped open, stunned, but all he said was, `Aye Sir.' He took his hand off the forty-five and Reyes let out a deep breath and went to welcome the ladies aboard and then took over as the Jg escorted them to the bridge.

Keoke was glad to see the Jg make an ass of, but in private protested the Captain's choice of words maintaining that he should have used the word ladies instead of women.

It wasn't long before the deal struck by Mary Soo and the Captain made the scuttlebutt chain of command. She would paint the ships sides and clean out the holds as much as was possible for so many pounds of rice, canned salmon and other goods from the ship's hold. These goods were to be conveniently logged as` lost at sea during unrep and therefore would not cost the ship anything and be well accounted for in the Navy's supply system.

Mary Soo was also allowed to run a soft drink concession on the deck, and they took over the duties in the scullery, dividing the food meticulously and then spiriting away the categorized garbage, much to the joy of Peaches and Doaks.

Her crews almost started at once cleaning and painting the sides of the ship, with long rollers and standing on wide log rafts. The crews were all men and the supervisors were all women. Mary Soo's outfit was matriarchal.

I had duty the first day, but Keoke, Heavy, and Bear even Reyes went over. Peaches and Doaks and Aqui had all been restricted. They were not prisoners-at-large. In port restriction meant that they were only restricted while in port. At sea they were free to roam the ship, except for Officer's Country, and places where they were not supposed to be. It was in this way that vindictive superiors could keep men on a ship, without ever leaving or going ashore for years. For example Peaches had been on the ship, restricted to it since before the ship left the States. The only time he'd been off the ship was emptying the trash on the pier in Alameda. Doaks, who had been able to go over in Subic was just now getting a taste of the restriction. Hong Kong lay there and they couldn't go over. Some guys went crazy.

I knew at least that I had the duty and tomorrow I'd have my chance to go over. That day I went to fantail, having no specific duty and just watch the junks and ferries plow through the waters of Hong Kong. It seemed as soon as one ferry past by another on would approach and pass by going the other way. From Hong Kong to Kowloon, what most of the sailors mispronounced as Calhoun. I watched the women and girls on the passing vessels with great interest. Some were dressed in the classic chi pao, the long slender dress with the long slit up the side of the thighs and the high neck. Others were more western styled dressed, but every vessel had beautiful women.

I stayed on the fan tail and ogled the Chinese, with their long silky hair and their almonds eyes, until dark then I chowed on fried rice delivered to the ship by a water taxi, then went back and watched the city lights come on. With the boats and ship and the lights of the city, Hong Kong was as pretty as San Francisco Bay, but warmer.

The Hatch team, those that were free, in dressed whites, filled the liberty barges and then motored to the wharf. Once on the beach, if they were lucky enough to have an overnight liberty, they hailed taxis and headed for the Wanchai district. It was the only place they knew the name of. If the Jg was that much against them going there, it had to be a pretty good place. When they rented a place in the cheap hotels they stipulated that their room must be above the first floor. In the midst of all that communist activity the enlisted men of the Topa apparently fit right in. Nobody noticed or bothered them.

By the time I got there the next day, Heavy had already negotiated and paid for a hotel room for as many nights as the Topa was going to be in port. It was a small, dirty place in a low class section of the Wanchai but after the cramped ship it seemed like a lot of real estate. There were free teas, brought hot by floor service, food or anything else could be ordered through Papa-san.

Heavy arranged for a wide variety of porno films to be shown, of which he had the cash to buy what he thought was the best for transportation and sales to the States, via his Uncle Sam's war ship. Beer came and we ate Chinese takeout food, fried rice in white boxes and with chop sticks, just like in the States, and drank and watched Heavy's potential films. It was a screening of sorts but all it made the men think about were women.

Keoke, Bear, Heavy sat around and watched the flicks and drank. There were even civilian clothes there and I changed into some jeans and a tee-shirt and was ready to hit the town.

Reyes and I left the digs and hit the streets.

Reyes was on the beach with a worried look. He was in a dark mood. He was going to try to call home. He wasn't sure what was wrong, but he'd written home to his parents and had received a reply, but there had been nothing from Alison, his wife. He wouldn't talk to me about it much. We found a telephone exchange and Reyes called. It rang and rang and rang until the operator broke in a told him to try again later.

"You might as well shove off Semmes. I'm going to hang around here and try to call back. It's early in the States now. She should be back later. No reason why you can't go off, have a good time, I'll catch you later." I said he would. Reyes waited and called, and called. He kept calling until it was three o'clock in the morning in the States then gave up and went back to the ship.

I on my own, walked around Hong Kong.

Doaks, Aqui and Peaches tried to sleep it off and not notice the men going over and coming back with all kinds of electronic gear and ornate carvings. Before the ship pulled out, one of the officers was to hoist a new small Chinese junk on board and put it in the hold for use back in the States. The sailors brought all kinds of goods down to the hold and one area was especially set aside for that purpose. On the second day, Peaches had had enough of restriction and had tried to climb the gunnel and drop himself into the harbor and swim to shore. The watch had caught him just in time, restrained him and then Doc had been called to give him a shot to put him asleep. He moaned and groaned that he was going over, he had to go over. He was carried down to his bunk but didn't stay there long. The next thing the watch knew he left his rack, come back on deck and had jumped over the side and was swimming in Hong Kong harbor in the direction of Hong Kong itself. Now almost all of those on the ship were on the main deck watching crazy Peaches refuse help from a passing junk. A bloated pig floated by on the tide. He kept swimming away from the junk and they kept trying to help him. Putting long poles and oars in the water.

One of the officers jumped off the fantail and started to swim for him. No sooner had the officer hit the water, than Peaches decided to give up and took a hold of one of the oars. The Chinese vessel came around and picked them up then brought them back to the ship. They were both wrapped in woolen blankets and

Peaches was given a double shot of tranquilizers and he wasn't any more trouble that day.

I went off by myself and walked around the streets of the city. They were crowded and I was soon lost in a market. People were hawking all kinds of vegetables, fruit and meat. There were normal stands and then every little area that was surrounding the market area also had vendors everywhere. Some of the fruits I had seen in Hue, but didn't know the Chinese names. I exited the market area and walked along the bustling streets. There were people everywhere.

I looked up and was greeted by a pair of round wire rim glasses. The black eyes behind the glasses were made larger by the moderately thick lenses. They sat on a nose that was not big by western standards but that flared enough at the nostrils to allow the specks to sit perfectly on her face, making her stunningly beautiful to me. There were rounded cheeks and thick eyes brows. She had a smallish mouth with almost full lips. They were a natural slash of red on her tanned face.

"American?" she asked.

"American."

"Then how come you dress like a Brit, sloppy old pants, baggy t-shirt, Shoes not bad." I was wearing my regulation cordovans. Half of her hair was combed back into a tight severe pony tail and gathered by a black oval piece of leather imprinted with a design and held there by a small dark wooden pole which protruded through the oval piece. The other half of her hair was combed forward and fell on her forehead and face in bangs that reached down toward the cheeks and made wispy false sideburns, and divided into two thick black shocks parted slightly on the right.

"I'm not a Brit, OK? I'm American, I'm from California."

A Chinese brushed by me and was carrying a box of lemons with "Saticoy Lemon Association" on the box. I couldn't believe it.

"There, look." I pointed to the box. "That box is from near where I'm from." She wrinkled her nose and squinted her eyes and looked at me like I was crazy. "Yes, maybe American."

"Not maybe, I ain't no limey."

"Then why so sloppy?"

"We dress like this in California." She grunted again. Then she brought up a book with long slender hands and pointed to a word.

I read it out loud to her. There were also Chinese characters in the work.

"You a student?"

"Yes, student, I study English, business, accounting. You help me O.K." It wasn't a question.

"Where do you study?" I asked her looking her over. She was young, maybe late high school or early college but she wouldn't pass for fifteen in the states except for her very serious countenance. She looked lithe and thin, but came almost up to my height and looked me in the eye when she spoke to me.

"Bo Zap Ban," It's a Cram school. You just come Hong Kong?" I nodded.

"I show you Hong Kong, you practice English with me." It was a business proposition with a heavily educational thrust.

"O.K."

"Where you want go first?"

"I don't know."

"We go Victoria tram." She turned and I followed her down the narrow street. I wanted to walk up alongside of her but that was impossible in the crowd so I trailed along behind her. We went up on the tram and looked over all of Hong Kong, and then to the beach, and finally that night went to the floating village. I had seen none of it before and it was all new and exciting for me. All the while she hung on my arm and engaged me in conversation. She stood so close to me that her small breast touched my arm and her hair brushed my shoulder and the rich chocolate like smell of her filled my nostrils.

The floating village was the best. We ate on a small junk, and then drank tea. We passed other little junks that had gambling on them. Some were stores others had musicians playing Chinese string instruments. Lovers cuddled and listened to the music. And still others were homes and young students were seen at their lessons. All the while she carried with her the concise English

Chinese dictionary and was constantly looking up words. I hefted the dictionary and looked through it. The most interesting parts for me were the maps of the U.S.A. and the U.K. On the American one I showed her where I lived. When the dinner on the vessel was over she took me back to the pier where I could catch the water taxi back to the ship. I wanted to kiss her good bye but she wasn't having any of it. I said good bye to the beautiful girl whose name I failed even to obtain and motored back to the ship. My mind was full of the things I'd seen and heard and smelled. If I didn't have it already, I was coming down with China fever. It was going to be hard to forget China.

A few days later Topa was back on line unrepping a bevy of horny fleet cans at twelve knots. Liberty felt like a thousand miles away, the States, and freedom, a forgotten dream. The endless days began and ended when ordered. The officers continued to walk around the ship in cool khaki shorts and in laundered and pressed uniforms. The old Samoan second class that ran the laundry would look at the sailors who passed his shack and say this.

"There's no water on this ship to drink, to shower, only for officer's uniforms. We lucky we got coffee."

The men went into the holds or worked on the deck and stood their watch and did all their duties. They slept in stinking crowded compartments, when they got the chance, slept in their bunks which hung on chains on the wall in the filth they had picked up from the engine room, or the holds, or from the deck, because there was no water for showers for the crew.

The food was tolerable when Robbie cooked, but nobody really paid attention. They were all too tired and fatigued.

I started to use chop sticks on the mess decks whenever there was anything that was cut up small enough. Heavy and Keoke joined me and Reyes on one of the small four man tables in the enlisted mess decks, for breakfast.

"Semmes, you been over here too long, you know that, you need some time in the States. Eating with chop sticks on the mess deck, boy you are going Asiatic on us."

145

"Look who's talking. How's your chit coming for getting married, did the Jg ever get it back to you?" Heavy pulled a chit out of his dirty dungaree pocket, opened it and then showed it to me and Reyes. Reyes, in a quiet deadly mood just looked at it, I said congratulations.

"Seems like the Jg, your buddy the Lt. Commander and the Captain were all sitting on the mother, till I called my congressman, and Anna called the British counsel. Seems like they both got hold of the ship on the same day. Man, the exec came down and personally gave me this mother, now all we gotta do is go back to Hong Kong so I can get married."

"Fat chance."

"We could do it in P.I., but it be better in the crown colony." I ate my scrambled eggs with my chop sticks to the stares of passing sailors.

"Talking about chits, my dad said that during WWII a sailor in his division's father died. The sailor put in a chit for emergency leave to go home for the funeral. Of course it was denied. Yet at the same time they were allowing officers to go home when their wives had babies. Well, the sailor was bummed out but what could he do? Then word came back from the States about a month later that the guy's mother had also passed away. He again put in for emergency leave and again it was denied. One morning my Dad said he went into the compartment and found the guy, hanging from the overhead. He committed suicide."

The 0500, morning chow was interrupted by the shrill whistle of the bosun's pipe.

"NOW HEAR THIS, NOW HERE THIS, SET THE UNDERWAY REPLENISHMENT DETAIL. HATCH TEAMS REPORT TO YOUR RESPECTIVE AREAS. HATCH TEAM LEADERS REPORT TO THE CARGO OFFICER."

The Filipino chief sat in his immaculate khakis and worked on the requests that had come from the ships that Topa would unrep, and translated the requests in to cargo orders for each hold.

Bear was there, his big frame hanging on a chair and his large hands holding his empty clip board in bored anticipation. His blue ball cap was set back on his large head. His face had the blue tinged, like Bruno in the Popeye cartoons, needing a shave.

The Jg came into the office and no body but the chief stood up. He looked around and focused on Bear.

"You need a shave, sailor." Bear smiled sheepishly at him. Then looked down and chuckled. Hee Hee, he shook his head back and forth.

"Here you are Bea." The chief said ending his scribbling with a flurry and whipping it out to Bear.

"Thanks chief, try to put an 'R' on the end of Bearrrrr, OK?"

I waited for my cargo order and looked out the porthole to see the early morning gray sea and the can that was pulling alongside of the Topa as she pounded through the swells. I could hear the P.A. system blare. ON THE TOPA, PREPARE TO RECEIVE SHOT LINE FORWARD, ON DECK, TAKE COVER.' Seconds later there was a boom, and another boom as the lines were shot across to the other ships so that the liaison could begin. The Jg came up to me.

"Semmes, you better buy some new uniform dungarees, those are pretty bad, almost unserviceable."

"I'd like to sir, but I've ready spent my four dollar and twenty cent clothing allowance on socks, sir." Bear and Bird snickered.

"Don't you think you should spend some of your own money on uniforms?"

"No sir." The chief turned around again, handing me the cargo break out. I took it put it on my clipboard and hurried out of the office and down to the hatch's square where my team waited. As I broke into the early morning light, away from the super structure, I checked the ocean's surface. It looked like Victory at Sea, there were ships everywhere waiting for their turn at the Topa: Carriers, Cans, may be a Cruiser.

When I got down to the square they had already broken into the hold securing the long hatch square covers off to the side and had climbed down, all except Heavy who was waiting for the clip board with the list. I threw him the clipboard and jumped down in the hold, scurrying over to the area where the first item was located. "The whole fleets up there. It's going to be a hell of a day."

I was right. We worked and worked and worked, receiving newer lists for different ships, brought into the hold by Pancho. The Jg would gleefully laugh at us from the relative safety of the main deck. He had nothing else to do.

Beat and tired, we were again the first team done and once secured I went to help Bear. On the main deck I could see that the carrier's deck loomed up and seemingly swung over towards Topa's.

Its' deck was so much higher than the Topa. They were already working on her. I paused just for a moment, coming out of the hold just to look at her. It was a mistake.

"Hold on sailor, I want to talk with you, you got a smart mouth, you know that, when I tell you, you ought to buy new dungarees yourself, you don't hand me any junk like you handed me today in the cargo office. If you do that again I'll have you up on charges and I'll make them stick, do you understand..."

The Jg went on and on and I just stood there taking the guff, but somehow knowing that I should be down in the hold helping the Bear and Peaches and Bubba and the rest of the team in number five. I stood there taking the chewing out for a long time when there were long pulls on the ship's horn.

I turned to see the carrier careening way too close for normal operations. The Jg started for the gunnel but I grabbed him and pulled him back, back away from the booms and the winches and toward safety. The horns continued and finally the word was given.

"BRACE FOR COLLISION. BRACE FOR COLLISION." In that moment the two ships smashed together, knocking me and the Jg to the deck. The ships scraped along each other for a second, metal screaming and cracking. Booms ripped from the masts and fell to the deck, shaking the ship like an earthquake. Topa shuttered and shook. Warning sirens blared. Topa jerked violently under the weight of the carrier's bulk. The decks shook beneath us.

I left the Jg on his ass and ran to the Bear's hold, across the wreckage on the deck. I saw the long gray hatch covers all over the hatch square below. They had come loose with the collision and had fallen like nails and had driven two of the hatch team down on the deck.

Bear and Peaches. Their hard hats sprawled among the cargo. Bear's head was at the wrong angle, the wrong angle for life. He lay there on the deck where he'd worked, where they all worked, worked for reliability during deployment, worked in support of the ships off the coast of Vietnam and the grunts ashore. Bear's soiled white shirt was ripped, his filthy dungaree pants disheveled. His big feet still. Bear wasn't going to move anymore, not by himself anyway.

Peaches lay there and tried to move, tried to get to the Bear but fell back unconscious. Bubba came over and began to dig Peaches and Bear out, throwing the hatch square covers off them, screaming their names again and again. The others called for Doc, who came running with his medical kit, and went down into the hold. Meanwhile on the deck the two ships fought to break away from one another. Lines were axed, booms secured again.

There was nothing Doc could do for Bear. Helicopters came from the carrier and medivacked Peaches and Bear to Da Nang Naval hospital. Peaches was transferred to Japan, Bear's body was flown home.

It was like the jar head marines had said in country Vietnam: if you get wounded, they'll get you to the Da Nang hospital in minutes, if it's bad they'll have you in Japan in hours, if you're dead, they'll get you home in a day.

The two ships separated. Topa assessed damage, tentatively heading for the Philippines. There hadn't been much, and the only two casualties had been Bear and Peaches. There was some structural damage.

Bubba, Keoke, Reyes, Heavy, Aqui, Doaks and me gathered around on the fantail than night in the abandoned gun tub and smoked a number. It could have been any of us down in the holds. It almost was.

"Lucky you didn't come down Semmes, you might be dead now." Bubba said.

"Or if I'd a come down sooner, you'd got done sooner, been out of the hold when it came down."

"Where were you anyway?"

"Being bitched out by the Jg on the main deck near the cargo office, I was coming to help, let me hit that joint." I took a long hard pull on the number and passed it to Reyes, who did the same and passed it to Doaks, then Keoke. There had been precious little left to do down there in the hold. They were on the last pallet load when the ships collided.

"I'd say he killed Bear, and hurt Peaches, just like he held a gun to them himself."

"He did kill them his-self."

"Look there." Reyes said. They all looked toward the super structure, past the masts and booms of hold number four and number five, Semmes and Bear's holds, and up on the 0-1 level. There was the Jg standing there, looking out to sea. From the abandoned gun tub aft, the sailors were at the same level as the officer on the 0-1 level, on the fringe of Officer's Country.

"He like to stand there don't he."

CHAPTER 8

Homeward Bound

The crew was in a bad very ugly mood and the meetings on the fantail on the abandoned gun tub became larger and larger once the sun went down. They met other places to, all along the deck, in closed lockers, and talked. But it was mostly centered in the abandoned gun tub.

The boys in Deck had caught a thief. The evidence was that he had a towel that belonged to someone else. The Division was the jury. The hanging judge was Big Red. They'd had thievery. The red haired seaman wouldn't admit it. He said it was all a big mistake. That he wasn't guilty. It didn't matter what he said. Big Red was going to extract punishment. He grabbed the seaman by the collar of his dungaree shirt and then smashed him against the bulkhead, picked him up and started slapping him across the face.

It looked like Big Red was beating up a miniature of himself. Big Red's hand got redder and redder, and blood was starting to show. The sailor's face was starting to puff up and bleed all over.

The Jg happened by.

"What's going on here." He growled.

"We caught a thief, sir."

The Jg just walked off. The beating continued, and continued.

The abandoned gun tub became the place of refuge. Before me and Reyes and Heavy and the others, Bear, and Doaks had been able to congregate there sometimes alone other times in pairs or threes and smoke a joint or just shoot the breeze. Now the number of sailors that went back there grew. They hooked up speakers to a music playing out fit and listened to rock in roll loudly. Led Zeppelin.

The number grew from two or three to twenty-five or thirty sailors. The gun tub was where Bear and Peaches had been air

151

lifted from. It was an area that the sailors controlled completely at night, like the forecastle used to be in the old sail ships. The big empty gun tub held memories of their shipmates. They never reached the P.I. The word came down the chain of command that the Topa was heading for COMCINCPAC; Commander in Chief Pacific. That was Pearl Harbor, Hawaii. There was going to be no more wild liberties in Subic or trips to anywhere else. The cruise was over for all practical purposes. All they had to do was get home.

Heavy was not going to get married overseas. He was going to have to have Anna come to the States, somewhere maybe Honolulu or the Frisco Bay. When he'd finally got the chit, the permission to get married, it had meant nothing. They were out to sea and moving away from Anna and mainland Asia. Now they were moving away from the Philippines as well.

This scuttlebutt put him at odds with Keoke who was overjoyed at the news, not that it could be believed too soon. It mattered to Reyes, he had not received letters and he had been unable to get a phone call through. He was desperate for knowledge but hid it well in his machismo. There were emotions he couldn't show, feeling he couldn't express.

Doaks could care less. The ship could sink as long as he got off in time. But it was nice to be going home. There would be leave and liberty and things American. It'd be nice to be back in the USA.

I was crazy. I was leaving Asia, all that good rice, and all those girls that would talk to you. I knew that I was going to have to make a decision. It was almost up, my hitch, my four years in the Navy after a life time of the military, of being born into the Navy, growing up on bases and studying at military school. I was going to have to cut it loose or ship over. Maybe I'd go to college and read a lot of books. Get an education so they can't take it away from you, learn to read and write so they can't tell you different. If I were truly rebellious, I would stay in the Navy and ship over. But if I was really obedient, obedient to my father, if I was really going to do my duty, then I would get out and go get that sheep skin diploma the Boats was always preaching about.

Aqui was pissed like Heavy, he'd been in the P.I., to his home and hadn't the chance to go ashore once. They headed straight for Pearl Harbor across the Pacific. The deck force began in earnest to do the deck ape work of making the decks shipshape, clean and maintenance after so many unrepps at sea and repair what they could from the collision.

There was going to be an inspection at Pearl. The Admiral's boys were going to come on board and see what the damage was and the condition of the ship. They wanted it looking nice. There was going to be an inquiry.

The Black gang in the engineer room tried to keep the Old Girl together and steaming east. In the now almost empty holds, the cargo division worked to clean them up, but every night, they would meet on the aft decks after ship's work had been secured and if they had no watch and smoke dope, drink, listen to music and complain.

Sometimes they could see the Jg on the deck, the 01 level of the superstructure, Officer's Country. They were on the same level now. Officers never walked the decks of the ships at night. It was the enlisted men who controlled the decks at night, at least aft of the super structure.

It was early in the morning the second day out to sea homeward bound from the collision. Aqui was doing the prep work for the day's chow in the officer's pantry. They were going far away from his home now, and with this ship going back to the States, and probably going to be decommissioned and sold off and scrapped, his orders would come and no telling where he'd go.

The officers were going to have stew for the noon chow so Aqui filled a large kettle with water, boiled it and then put it on simmer when he had an idea. He had to piss. He got a stool and stood on it, overlooking the officer's soup. He was going to make it a sweet and sour stew. The officers would love the exotic Oriental fare. With one hand he steadied himself on the overhead. With the other he undid his pants. He took his thing in his hand. He felt the urine coming to the head. He aimed his dark penis at the kettle and soon there was the sound of the urine topping off the officer's stew. It drowned out the hum and cries of the ship. The steam from the boiling pot and the steam from his piss, warm and yellow colored and commingled.

The door opened and the Jg stood there and watched as Aqui finished pissing in their stew. Aqui knew he was busted and just smiled as he buttoned up his pants and hopped down from the stool to the deck of the pantry. The Jg quickly disappeared but would return later with other senior officers to write up Aqui. But there had been no witnesses, and Aqui denied it. Aqui had dumped it. There wasn't much that could be done, court martial wise, but the captain had contacted a ship going the other way, a small destroyer, trying to get to the Tonkin Gulf and asked if they need a steward as they were just starting a long West Pac deployment.

Their C.O. said "Sure." and about mid-day the Destroyer came along side, the deck team was mustered, shot lines were fired across and connected up and Aqui was transferred, like the crew had transferred cargo, but in a little bosun's chair. In route across the sea between the two ships a rogue wave reared up, and someone on the Topa slacked the line. Aqui was smashed by the ocean swell and drenched in the little wire cage of a chair.

The crew was wild with the scuttlebutt how Aqui had been found pissing in the Officer's stew by the Jg., and so transferred quickly. It was the rage of conversation below decks and in every compartment and gathering area. The big question was how long had Aqui been pissing in the officer chow? How long had he made the officers eat urine, without them knowing it and them not ever suspecting that their docile Filipino man servant were stabbing them in the back at every turn.

The crew in general looked up to Aqui from this point. He was seen in new respectful terms. If the crew could give medals, Aqui would have received one for audacity, for pissing in the officer's food. It was too rich. Suddenly all the stewards were suspect by the officers, and admired by the enlisted men.

I never saw Aqui after he was released from the little boatswain's chair and helped below decks wet and cold but somehow triumphant like a little Irish rebel ready to be hung on the banks of the Bann River. The Ships broke away in the rolling gray seas. The Topa continued for the States, the little destroyer made for the Tonkin. Aqui wasn't going to be seeing any liberty for a long, long time.

The ship steamed for Hawaii, and the crew took even more control at night. The get together on the fantail, in the abandon gun tub grew in size. The sailors listened to their music and watched the stars and rolled with the ship alone in relative freedom.

During the days, the short timers, those who would be discharged as soon as the Topa hit port walked around the ship yelling and screaming about how many days they had.

"Twenty-one days and it's your Navy." Nobody answered them. Nobody except the guys who maybe thought they had less days. They were jubilant and cocky.

There was a sea bag inspection. They wanted to make sure everybody had a complete bag of Navy regulation clothes. The Jg was the inspecting officer. He came rarely enough into the smelly crowded crew berthing quarters. The whole Supply Department was there and not being in the bunks on the wall, as they were when they slept and being all on the deck, with their bags in prep for the inspection, they stood closer than shoulder to shoulder and had to bunch up.

The khaki uniformed Jg had to move, with his little clipboard, among the sea of dungaree. He was uncomfortable and at a disadvantage. You could see it in his face. Gone was the confidence and condescending manner he showed on payday when he countered out the cash to the dumb sailors.

The crew made the inspection a farce. As the items were called out, and as the Jg looked and counted the clothing, items from one bag were placed in another. The Jg came to Bird, a short timer who was getting out as soon as the ship tied up in Alameda. He would be in the first liberty call, but with his sea bag packed and his blues ready he was not going to be going just on liberty, or on leave. He would have a nice honorable discharge and travel pay to the East Coast of the U.S.A. Travel money. Why would Bird want to buy additional Navy clothing that he might never have to use?

"Socks, six pair." the Jg called out.

"Socks, six pair." Bird returned, but in a loud booming voice, holding up two fingers. He meant his bag was light two pairs. He only had four pair and was requesting two additional pair. I quickly provided them surreptitiously.

The Jg looked up from the clipboard and counted six pair, then called the next item, looking down again and the fiasco was repeated until everybody had passed the bag inspecting, although few had a full bag. The same items were countered again and again by the unknowing Jg.

The ship left the humid Asian mainland influences and drew closer to Hawaii the weather turned from hot to glorious little by little. When the weather seemed perfect, the Topa slipped through the narrow mouth of Pearl Harbor and docked. The story was that the ship would be decommissioned in the Islands, but it proved false. Inspectors came and the captain went ashore to visit COMCINCPAC. Surely there was an inquiry into the collision and the death of the Bear and Peaches getting injured. It was kept quiet. No one in supply was called to testify.

The only thing I did was to take Reyes surfing. We took a taxi from the base to Waikiki and rented a hotel room for the day. All we carried were towels and our regulation bun hugger swimming trunks.

We could both feel the stares of the civilians as we walked down the heart of Waikiki in our uniforms and rented a place to stay. We were welcomed like participants in the My Lai Massacre. The little motel proper was filled with mainland tourist types, and with one look at us, sailors in uniform they would turn away, gasp in alarm and flee. Maybe they thought Reyes and I burned villages and killed babies.

"Welcome come back to America," I thought. We went into the room and changed into swimming trunks, rented some boards and went and surfing at a place called "Number Threes" right in front of Fort Derussy. One of the few places I had surfed on R and R from Viet Nam.

I sat on the rented board and watched the wave smoking white with the brisk off shore approach my position, I thought the war was winding down, Vietnamization and peace with honor were in the air, as was My Lai. CYA, brother, CYA, cover your ass.

There wasn't going to be any real investigation by the Navy about how the Bear died. By the time a real investigation could be mounted the ship's crew would be scattered to the four winds. Most would be civilians and bringing them back would be nightmarishly impossible. It was only Bear and Peaches, after all, a half Oregon Indian logger and drunk and a homosexual cook, nothing really important. Not to the Navy anyway. They we just enlisted men.

The wave came closer and I turned the board around and stroked toward the shore. The swell lifted me up and windblown spray pulverized my face until I was to my feet and dropping down its face to the bottom. Then I could see and turned along the wave's wall and raced forward until the wave smashed me off my fragile foothold. I swam for the board in the soupy warm water of Waikiki. I was enjoying the freedom of the wave riding experience and paddled out to do it again.

It was in Hawaii that word came down to the Topa that Peaches had died of his wounds. He had never regained consciousness. Bubba was pissed and he and Keoke, who had been determined not to leave the Islands again, went over to the base club the last night in Pearl for some brewskis. Bubba was pissed and sobbing in his beer about Peaches when somebody, one of the Pearl Harbor home ported boys said something. Bubba jumped him and Keoke, screamed.

"Kill Haole, kill haole." He jumped into the fray. It took twenty Shore Patrol to quell Bubba and Keoke and in the process many were hurt badly, and the Enlisted men's club was in ruin. The base commanding admiral wasn't amused. A summary court martial was set for Keoke and Bubba. They were going to spend a long time in the brig, then get discharged, but at least for Keoke it was going to be a Hawaiian brig.

When the Topa pulled out the next day her big Hawaiian deck ape and her African-American line cook stayed behind for court martial.

Reyes, the last night in Pearl, had gone over to the phone exchange and called home. He put the coins in the machine, got the operator and gave her the number and the area code. He had a lot of coins standing by. He wasn't going to be cut off. He tried to figure the time. There was a couple-three hour difference. He wanted her to be there. He needed to talk to Alison. If there was trouble, it was O.K. They could work out. He would try to forgive anything. He loved her more than he could tell anyone, and would do anything for her. All she had to do was to tell him what she wanted to do. All she had to do was to be there for him to talk to.

The number was connected and rang three times before a recording came on.

"The number you dialed…. has been disconnected and is no longer in use. Please consult your directory for the new listing."

He jerked the phone and the operator came back on the line. He was frantic and angry, and asked her to dial the number again. This time she stayed on the line with him. They heard the same recording together. She asked him if he wanted to go to directory assistance. He said yes, but working together for the next few minutes in the Bay area failed to produce a new number for Alison. He left the phone exchange stunned and walked back to the ship. "I'll find her when Topa gets back to Alameda," he pledged to himself, but not sure anymore what he would find there.

The Pacific got colder and colder as the ship pulled away from Hawaii and got closer and closer to North America and the San Francisco Bay area. The nights got chilly and the crowds that met on the deck after chow, got smaller and smaller. Some now picked areas to go that were more enclosed, like lockers and shacks. These filled up quickly and joints and booze were passed around.

Me and Reyes and Heavy still met, sometimes with Doaks, who had never been relieved mess cooking, and was plenty busy and always beat, on the fan tail gun tub to smoke a joint and talk. We would get high and then retreat to Reyes' ship fitter shack and shoot the bull.

Keoke's departure from the ship had been a financial disaster for Heavy. The sailors who had borrowed money from Heavy, and who had feared Keoke, now laughed at Heavy alone.

"Try and get the money back, I ain't afraid of you." Heavy didn't have the muscle himself and no one was interested in helping. Heavy had made a good profit already on the voyage but from the time of Keoke's fight in the Enlisted men's Club in Pearl, the outstanding loans on the Topa were a write off.

Reyes was in a dark pensive mood since he'd tried to call Alison. He turned bitter. Swearing oaths of vengeance, and running her down in his own mind but never to his shipmates.

One morning Doaks refused to get up early for mess cooking duties. At 0500 the new cook striker, the guy who replaced Peaches, came in to roust out the mess cooks. Doaks refused to get up. A couple of minutes later a second class cook came down and wrote up Doaks for failure to obey a direct order.

In the cargo office, a few days later, Bird, the short timer, asked the Jg what Doaks was going to get. In the Naval jurisprudence of the time, the one who would act as the prosecutor, and the man who would act for the defense were the same officer, the man's boss. So it wasn't a case of guilty or innocent, it was always a case of personalities. That's what determined how much the punishment was going to be. There would be no innocent judgments. There would be no mitigating circumstances unless the officers who were running the show felt the need to mention them. Nobody was going to do that for Doaks. The captain of a Naval ship had the power, without going to any high authority, to punish a man with brig time and a bad conduct discharge. The Jg knew this.

"I'm all for Doaks." the Jg said.

"I'm recommending SIX MONTHS HARD LABOR, SIX MONTHS CONFINEMENT AND A BAD CONDUCT DISCHARGE."

The men looked at one another slowly then slightly shook their heads, pensively peering at their knees. It had been written up as disobeying a direct order, but all Doaks had really done was to get up a few minutes late after months of prejudicial treatment. He had gotten up. He had gone and done the duty. For that, he was getting six months hard labor then six months confinement, a year in jail, in a Navy brig, and then a bad discharge. His whole life was going to be ruined.

This was the power they feared. This was the power the officers had over them. A short time later, Doaks' court martial went just as the Jg had predicted and Doaks was to be taken off the ship in chains by marine guards as she docked in the Bay and remanded to Naval Justice system. Till that time he was a prisoner at large, still expected to do his duty as a mess cook and report so many times a day.

Reyes, Heavy and the others could barely believe it.

"This is Naval Justice." I said.

"It's about time we got some justice." Someone mumbled. It was a threat.

Bird and Pancho, who were being discharged as soon as the Topa hit port, tried to put me up for second class one morning with the Jg.

"Ain't Semmes eligible for second class, sir.

"Yes, sir ain't that right."

The Jg looked at me then back at the two short timer second classes. "Yes he is eligible, but he'd have to extent for nine months."

I just sat there, lowered my head and smiled.

It was a day out of San Francisco and the weather had turned cold and foggy. The gray seas under and the white caps no longer looked inviting at daily morning quarters and the men were wearing again the naval blue jacket as the uniform of the day. The stiff cold winds and the speed of the ships caused the men to pull their hats down tight and put their little blue collars up against the cold.

The Topa was close to home and in such a hurry, that the officers decided to dump the excess fuel oil in the Pacific. It would take too long to off load it.

Once through the gate they were going to have to go to Port Chicago to off load ammo. Then they could make their homeport of Alameda. Home port for some happy ones meant discharge. For others it meant transfers, and for others the brig. It was close to being over.

The word passed through the ship what punishment Doaks had copped. To some he was just another worthless sailor, obviously he was that to the officers. But to Reyes, me and Heavy, who had humped with him in the holds, sweated with him, slept near him, and showered with him, ate with him, he was a brother. His arbitrary punishment could be ours too.

Reyes started figuring some white boy, some officer type, no better than the Jg was dicking Alison. He was ready for revenge.

Heavy was going through a financial disaster. The cruise that had started so well was crumbling all around him. Although he'd got the permission chit approved to marry the Chinese Filipina Anna, but he was far away from her.

I didn't want to do anything to jeopardize my Honorable Separation, but I felt there had to be some kind of retribution.

"Let's off the Jg." Somebody said. He hit a 'J' and passed it. The wind blew cold and hard but the three sailors sat there, in the gun tub talking, and huddled close together against the cold Northern Pacific.

"Let's do it."

"How?"

"I got a plan. Man comes on the 0-1 level every night for he hits his rack. We dump him overboard. He's in supply. Nobody will notice him for maybe eight hours. They won't go back one hundred twenty miles to look for him."

Reyes saw the Jg come out of Officer's Country and stand on the 0-1 level, starboard side. Reyes left the gun tub and ran forward on the port side and silently flew up the ladder and approached the hatless Jg from the rear.

The Jg turned around just a Reyes reached him. The strong ship fitter pushed the officer with all his might and pinned up furry, upward from where the officer's ribs sank into his stomach.

The officer grunted and flew backwards, stumbling over the rail and falling towards the cold night's black churning Pacific Ocean.

Reyes barely caught himself at the rail. The last thing he saw of the Jg were the eyes of his hatless head, full of surprise falling, falling away, in terror.

No one even heard a splash among the noises of the sea and ship at night. Reyes returned to the gun tub.

"You did it."

"Don't funk around." They waited for a good minute to see if the fan tail watch would see the Jg and sound, MAN OVER BOARD, but there was nothing.

"Maybe he got sucked into the screws."

"It doesn't matter now."

"Semmes, do me a favor."

"Depends."

"There'll be some heat about this and we got to take it off us."

"He's right."

"We gotta cover our ass."

"Plant some dope in his state room."

"You mean go to Officer's Country, carrying dope?"

"Yeah, with some dope, hide it there."

"Why me?"

"You know where his stateroom is, he's bitched you out enough times there. He caused Bear's death bitching you out."

"And Peaches' too."

"How about Aqui,"

"And Doaks."

"The Jg's gone but we still gotta cover our ass." Reyes and Heavy looked at Semmes.

"Give me the dope."

I took the dope, a few joints in a plastic baggy, tucked it in my blue jacket and walked into the superstructure of the ship. The best way to Officer's Country would be to go up from the bowels of the ship. I paused near the stairs that went up to Officer's Country, and listened for any sounds, or movement. There was none. The watch

162

would not be relieved for an hour and mid rats for the watch had already been prepared, and set out.

I edged my way up the ladders, listening ever so carefully, but once in the passageway moved quickly around the corner and down its length to the end where the Jg's state room was. The doors were generally closed and the curtains drawn to all the rooms. I slipped past the curtain and entered the Jg's stateroom. With one person in the room it looked spacious. His hat, the gold banded officer's cap, lay on the bunk. I stared at it for a moment then looked around. Where to hide the dope? I slipped the plastic baggy with the few joints under the Jg's pillow.

Someone was moving down the passageway. I froze as the steps on the deck moved closer and closer. A near door opened and closed. The sound of movement boomed in my ears but gradually faded. If I got caught here and they found the Jg missing it be Portsmouth Naval prison for life, maybe even execution on a murder rap. I tried to control my breathing, and my heart pounded so loud I was sure it could be heard in San Francisco.

It had been quiet for a long time when I exited the stateroom and moved swiftly and silently down the passageway to the ladders that led back to the main deck. I slid down and left the superstructure for the main deck aft.

The next morning, before muster, word was passed, during chow, from the watch reliefs, down from the Topa's bridge that the ship was approaching San Francisco's Golden Gate. Sailors, the short timers, and the hopefuls ran on deck with their white hats. As tradition had it among the sailors on the Topa, if a sailor threw his white hat at the bridge, and the hat fell into the water, the sailor would make no more West Pacs. But if the hat fell back on the deck, then the sailor was destined to return to Asia.

Heavy stumbled on deck with the rest and flung his hat high into the gray fog that swirled around the ship and the rust colored, fog shrouded gate. His hat plopped back on deck, and as Heavy saw it hit, his face turned white. He ran to the hat, picked it up and flung it again with all his might toward the Golden Gate Bridge. It disappeared into a swirl of fog and Heavy returned to the warmth of the superstructure and did not see his hat land back on the deck again.

I did not throw my hat, I knew I would be going back to Asia. Reyes threw his hat and saw it hit the water and float for just an instant and then sink beneath the waves. It's the happiest I had seen him for a long while.

Later at quarters, the word was being passed for the Lieutenant Jg. to report to the bridge. The Chief Master at Arms and the First Lieutenant made a search of the ship for him. Then nothing was heard. The scuttlebutt later that morning was that the Jg's hat had been found on his bunk, and some dope had been found too. They surmised that the officer had gotten loaded and then fallen overboard last night at sea. It would have been useless to go back for the man. It had been ten hours.

A board of inquiry was convened and concluded accidental death. The planted dope took the heat off the crew. It was an easy explanation. For murder there were just too many suspects.

The ship did not go to Alameda but went up to Port Chicago where she off loaded ammo and spent the night. The news came down the pipe indirectly that the ship was to be decommissioned. A load of orders came in for those sailors who were not to be discharged. They would be going to other ships.

Leaves were canceled but early outs were announced of up to three months. Bird and Pancho would be getting out as soon as the ship hit homeport. Others already had orders. Pappy for one had been on the ship for eight years in the engine room and was all but deaf. He had been on her when the Topa had been home ported out at Sasebo, Japan. His leave started at 0001 hours, the night we moored off Port Chicago. The last liberty barge left Topa at 2345, and there would not be another until 0600 in the morning. Happy put in a special request to leave the ship fifteen minutes early and thus save six hours of travel time. The request was denied. It was denied after eight years aboard the ship and a lifetime in the navy. The crew knew immediately, they were not surprised. They shook their heads.

"That's how they treat lifers, can you imagine how they'll treat you."

"I'm glad I'm getting out."

From Port Chicago the wives and dependents and family member were alerted to the fact that the Topa was back, so they could organize a homecoming. It was time to kick the marine out, the sailor was coming home. We came home and the small group of wives and loved ones was waiting. Heavy, Reyes and I manned the rails, but no one was there to meet us. I had the duty and the watch later that night, the gangway in-port quarterdeck watch, so I couldn't go over.

As the ship gangplank touched the dock in Alameda, Marine Corp guards came aboard to transport Doaks to the brig, shackled and handcuffed for his year of bad time.

Reyes went on the dock, among the happy families, before the ships telephones were hooked up and tried to call Alison. The number had been given to someone else. They'd never heard of her. She'd disappeared. As he was coming back aboard ship, a man in a suit met Reyes.

"Are you Ship fitter Third class Reyes?" The man asked in a polite friendly way.

"That's right." The sailor said surprised.

The man handed him a legal paper that said he was being sued for divorce. Reyes came back on board with the document. He couldn't read much of it through his tears, but he knew it was over. That night Reyes had liberty, went over, and looked through the abandoned apartment that they had rented. The landlady looked scared when he questioned her. She didn't know anything. Yes, a man had lived here a very short while then they had moved out. Reyes didn't know what to do. He came back to the ship.

The next day Reyes had the 2000 to 2400 quarterdeck watch, but before he assumed the watch Reyes, me and Heavy smoked a joint in the gun tub. Just like old times. Reyes was finally talking. Everybody knew about the divorce anyway.

"I been trying to get a hold of her, I can't even find her. I think she's somewhere up in Berkeley. I tried to call her family, they won't say a thing."

"If I go to Berkeley to look for her everybody will think I'm a cop." He made a motion with his hands indicating his short hair.

"Nobody would talk to me. It'll work out somehow. How can it work out, there's no hope for us, or for me."

There wasn't much we could say to him. Heavy's girl was in Asia. He was facing the same thing. My old girlfriend had broken up with me before I went to Nam. But it had only been a girl, for both of us, not a wife.

We broke up, loaded, Heavy and I went to our racks. Reyes assumed the watch on the in port quarter deck.

There were a lot of empty bunks as the crew size had been diminished with discharges and transfers, there were new faces just come aboard. For them the Topa was little more than a transit barracks. They were only on her for the decommissioning.

Two hours later, right near taps, Heavy and I were both awakened from a bad sleep by the loud pop of small arms coming from the main deck above. Then the word was being passed by the messenger of the watch for the O.D. to report to the quarterdeck ASAP, along with the Master at Arms, and the Corpsman. Heavy looked up and caught my eye. We rolled out of our bunks and down the chains. We got dressed then went to the main deck, to the quarterdeck, but the Chief Master at Arms blocked our way. We could just peer down the passageway and see Reyes' body, with the back of his head blown away, sprawled on the deck. The heavy black forty-five we had all carried on watch was sprawled near his hand.

"Get out of here." the O.D. said chasing us away. Back on the fan tail gun tub Heavy produced a joint. I tested the wind. We found a place on the old Topa where the smoke would blow harmlessly away in the night sky and not be detected. Heavy lit the jag, his hands trembled as he took an expansive hit and passed it to me.

"He was a good guy. He didn't have to do that."

"Yeah, now his wife gonna pick up 10,000 bucks if they rule it an accident." The Navy did so rule.

The ship decommissioning work lasted for a month, and the old girl was stripped down and made ready for death. I would be like a boy going from his mother. She had to let me go. She would go to her death, being decommissioned and struck, handed over to the Maritime Administration and sold for scrap to the Koreans. During the last weeks on the ship I was in a bad mood and angry with everybody and everything. I had gone home, taking the greyhound and picked up my van. I bought a new surfboard.

I stood the last mid watch with some Puerto Rican seaman I'd never seen before. There was also a crisp young educated just graduated from college Ensign. Two dudes I didn't want to talk to. I had nothing to say. I was a short timer, but I would never say it. Never say it because by doing so, I thought I might jinx my bid for freedom, my chance.

It was a little into the watch, just after 2400 when Heavy appeared on deck with his sea bag slung over his shoulder balanced by one hand and a manila envelope in the other hand. He sat the bag down and walked over to me. Heavy had new bright red second class stripes on his arm and a new red hash mark on his forearm! I looked at the hash mark on Heavy's arm and the two red stripes below his pristine white crow. Heavy had made second class and shipped over. I could barely believe it. Heavy had shipped over.

"Orders to my new ship." He smiled pointing to the manila envelope. "I was supposed to leave at 2400 but I thought I'd give the old girl five more minutes of my time."

I sneered at the fresh ensign and then walked over to Heavy with my hand stuck out. Heavy grabbed it and we embraced for a long moment, fighting back the tears that welled up and then looked at each other. We could only act angry.

"Good luck."

"What? No recriminations for shipping over, no lifer jive?"

"Congrats on making second class, Heavy."

"Yeah, Semmes, I'd always figured YOU for the lifer, when all the time it was ME. There's just so many ways to make money, how I'm going to do that on the outside unless I work my ass off? Plus I gotta get back to Anna, she's waiting for me in Subic."

We both laughed, but there was something between us, something that wasn't there before. I could understand a career in the Navy although I wanted something else, a chance for school. We knew we'd never see one another again.

"I guess this is it?"

"Take care of yourself, you friggen lifer."

"Hey sailor, you take of yourself too."

I gave Heavy a tap for good luck on the arm. Heavy hoisted the sea bag back on his shoulder.

"Sir," he said to the ensign in a loud and booming voice, "Permission to leave the ship as ordered." The ensign signed him out and permission was granted. I watched Heavy the new second class career man walk down the accommodation ladder. Just as he reached the bottom I yelled out.

"Hey stores, don't you ever call me "Sailor" again." I sounded pissed.

"Semmes, you'll always be a loud mouth sailor, nothing will change that, it's in your blood."

And then Heavy walked off into the darkness and the haze gray fog, heading down the pier and for his leave and then his new ship.

EPILOGUE

The decommissioning ceremony for the old gal Topa was held a few days later, and happened about the time of the first National moratorium against the War in Vietnam, October 15th, 1969. There were parades and demonstrations against the war everywhere, including right outside the Alameda's main gate. A stiff chilly early morning and early winter wind whipped off the San Francisco Bay, and blew stronger all day, wrinkling the Bay's face and that of the mud flats that lay in back of Alameda, and formed white caps everywhere. The skeleton crew, many of them new to the Topa, mustered at hold number three, on the main deck just forward of the super structure under deep blue clear skies punctuated with white puffy clouds that raced by overhead.

Some captain, a four striper, I had never seen before, spoke at the decommissioning ceremony. There were a lot of new faces and nameless officers at the muster. I felt alone, not part of them or of the ceremony.

The Topa was the men long gone who had sweated and struggled in the holds of the ship during the underway replenishment off the coast of Viet Nam, men like the Bear, and Peaches, now dead. Men like Aqui and Doaks, who fought each other but still worked together, who were now in exile or in a tough Naval Prison. Men like Keoke, home at last, but in a Navy brig. Men like Reyes, the faithful, who was involved with a woman who wasn't, in a time of change and doubt, whose final solution was to put the barrel of a forty-five to his head. And men like Heavy, who turned out to be a lifer. Who was now on leave but would serve the Navy on other ships.

These men, who had worked within the Topa, they were gone, and the men that remained were nothing to me.

The only thing I still knew there was the ship. I looked around at her for the last time. There was a tough, heavy knot in my chest.

We both had no choice. I set my face in a scowl, narrowed my eyes and bit my cheek. Some of the old ones were still there, the Lieutenant Commander, the first lieutenant, a few snipes, a deck ape, a yeoman. The rest were gone, as soon I would be too. Soon Topa herself would be no more.

I looked down at my honorable separation papers and then to the crow on my arm and knew that the long haul would soon be over. I wore the uniform of a defeated Navy and the shoulder patch of a ship being struck from the Navy list. But I still had my keys, those cross keys which sat under the white eagle, my crow. I had nothing to go back to in the outside but had to see what it was like being free. I realized there would be no victory parades, no slaps on the back, no girl waiting. There was only a hostile antiwar crowd who thought me evil and my service of no account. My only defense would be silence. Even though I had written "C" Street, Ventura, California on my ditty bag, I knew that there was no home to go back to, I was leaving the only home I had really ever known. I also knew that I would never really be free of the ship, never free of navy, where I had literally grown up. That would stay with me forever. Heavy's words rang in his ears. 'Semmes you'll always be a loud mouthed sailor. Nothing will change that. It's in your blood.'

Soon the speech was over. I had not heard a word and would remember nothing of it in the years to come. After "Dismissed" was ordered, I took an about face and was officially free. I started to walk away. The Lieutenant Commander was in my path. The Commander offered his hand to me. I hesitated.

"Come on Semmes, give me a hand shake." I remember the good things about the Commander, and reached my hand out and shook his hand. The Commander's said 'Good Luck, Semmes." I said nothing. I swept past the Commander and fled the main deck then went down the gang way to the pier. I saluted nothing because the hulk ceased to be the Topa, ceased to be a ship with a quarter deck watch or a flag. Once on the pier I hurriedly walked toward the van that was packed with my sea bag and surfboard, got in and started the engine and drove toward the gate. I didn't look back.

At the gate, the base's entrance, there were hundreds of antiwar people demonstrating and chanting. I drove past them flashing the peace symbol. They cheered. I turned south and drove along the edge of the San Francisco Bay, passed through San Jose and then traversed the long narrowing Salinas valley.

The stars overhead were a bright canopy, like being at sea, on the road through the highlands of Paso Robles and Atascadero. On the big grade before San Luis Obispo I left the stars and descended into a blanket of sea grayish white fog pressing tight up against the coastal valleys and towns.

I only stopped for gas and coffee. I wore the uniform into the little restaurants and took the sneers and catcalls from the civilians. I could careless now. I chugged at fifty miles an hour in the old van, the van I'd bought with the money saved humming ammo in Vietnam.

Every once in a while I would slide back the window, stick my head out and scream into the black star filled night. It felt good. Other times on the long drive south I wept. The wind whipped me around going through the Gaviota pass and into the Santa Barbara Channel.

Past Santa Barbara, down from Carpinteria on the Rincon, at a lonely beach break just north of San Buenaventura I pulled off the side of the road and climbed in the back and took off my uniform for the last time. I'd been sitting in it since the decommissioning. The white hat was first, I folded it up as I would all the uniform, regulation style, inside out, like I'd done my whole life, and then sat it on the back seat. The black neckerchief, the dark blue thirteen chances to say no bell bottomed trousers, the uniformed blouse, with the Topa's name on the right shoulder and my cross keys below the eagle and above my third class stripe on the left shoulder. Crossed American flags hidden beneath the piping on the cuffs. Finally I took off the black cordovan regulation low cuts and the black socks. They all came off for the last time.

I then took my waxed up surfboard out of the car and sat next to it, on the beach and watched the sun come up on the rest of my life.

The waves looked small but perfect, perhaps coming from a late southern storm far, far away. I picked up the board and walked to the waiting lonely surf. The water was surprisingly warm and inviting. A hot Santa Ana wind rushed down past the chaparral and blew the tops of the waves off, like white smoke, the plumes headed for Asia. I waded in and paddled my board outside to the waiting roaring surf. I was free and home.

-The End-

ABOUT THE AUTHOR

Mr. Yenney is a Vietnam veteran who has a few hobbies; one of them is writing. He is currently a resident of Ventura County. West Pac is his second novel.

CPSIA information can be obtained
at www.ICGtesting.com
Printed in the USA
FSOW02n0051140415
6424FS